Get In My Swamp

An Ogre Love Story

G.M. Fairy

G.M. Fairy

Copyright © 2023 by G.M. Fairy

All rights reserved.

FIRST EDITION

To anyone who feels like they have as many layers as an onion.

Content Warning

Get In My Swamp is a dark fantasy romance between a snarky young woman and a brute green ogre. While fun, the story includes elements that might not be suitable for some readers. Abduction (non-consensual bondage), consensual bondage, incest, mention/description of past trauma (child abuse, neglect, suicide), cheating, and violence are present in the novel. Readers who may be sensitive to this content, please take note.

Contents

1. Liona   1

2. Beck   9

3. Liona   13

4. Liona   18

5. Beck   23

6. Beck   30

7. Liona   39

8. Beck   50

9. Liona   59

10. Liona   67

11. Beck   78

12. Liona   82

13. Beck   91

14. Liona   97

15. Beck   105

16. Liona   114

17. Beck   127

18. Liona   132

19. Beck   143

20. Liona   148

21. Liona   152

22. Liona   157

23. Liona   167

24. Beck   173

25. Liona   180

Thanks for reading!   186

CHAPTER ONE

Liona

Most young women don't imagine their bachelorette party at a swamp in the middle of bumfuck-no-where Florida. Most women also don't imagine being surrounded by a gaggle of females so dissimilar from themselves that they wonder if they're even the same species.

But alas, I'm not most women. I am Liona Granger, the unluckiest woman there is.

As if being in a swamp wasn't bad enough of a bachelorette trip, I'm here at a silent retreat.

Victoria Farque is the only human being I know that would think it's a good idea to hold a bachelorette party in such a place. I'm fortunate to have Victoria Farque as not only my maid of honor but also my future sister-in-law. Yay, me.

To be fair, Victoria is halfway decent. Although her passive-aggressive comments about anything I own that's not vegan or humanely sourced make me want to jump off a cliff, she did take me under her wing when I started dating her brother.

I was a loser nobody, working as a waitress at The Clover, a semi-boujee restaurant in town. I had no friends or family when Lawrence Farque came into my life and flipped everything upside down. Actually, Lawrence *and* Victoria flipped my life upside down since she's the one who took me shopping, brought me to every LA social gathering worth attending, and helped me become the sister-in-law she always dreamed of. Well, at least as much as she could.

I should be thankful for her. I know I should, but right now, I am sitting on a stone floor in a hut with no air-conditioning, surrounded by a group of girls that have never worked a day in their lives, and we're all just staring at each other. In silence.

"I'm bored," I whisper to Ellie next to me.

She's one of Victoria's best friends, and she's been a common occurrence among our social gatherings ever since I started dating Lawrence. I think I've only ever said twenty words to her directly, but apparently, she's close enough to me to be an attendee on my bachelorette trip.

Ellie says nothing. She just looks at me like a lamb about to be slaughtered. She's a rule follower, and I know that I always make her uncomfortable.

"Sorry!" I now say without even trying to whisper.

The other three girls, Hannah, Rachel, and Polly, all look at me with similar petrified glares. Victoria and the instructor of this silent mindfulness session shoot me a death stare.

Since we arrived here yesterday, I've broken the "no talking" rule about seventy times. I'm pretty sure if I keep this up, someone will murder me.

I'm the bride, aren't I? Shouldn't I be allowed to break rules at my own bachelorette party?

Obviously, this trip is not the trip of my dreams. I'm pretty sure Victoria planned it so that she could stop having to listen to my lame dad jokes for a week. But I do feel like this trip fits the theme of the wedding because if I'm being honest with myself, which I am in the mood to do right now (I think this mindfulness is working), this wedding is not the wedding of my dreams.

I don't mean the flowers, the catering, or the dress, although all of those are more of Victoria's taste than mine. I mean the groom.

Ah, how does one describe Lawrence Farque? Actually, pretty easily because he is as bland and stereotypical as a three-ingredient recipe. He's rich, obviously, and most importantly. He's the heir of the mighty Dual-Lock home security empire, and it's surprisingly a very profitable industry.

He's nice. We'll nice-ish. He's polite and professional to everyone he meets, but behind their backs will tear them apart like he's Chef Gordon Ramsay and everyone is just an idiot sandwich. I know he probably talks shit about me too. I have my fair share of shit to talk about. I assume Victoria is at the receiving end of his shit-talking and probably partakes in the activity herself.

Lawrence and Victoria aren't twins, but you might think they are. They try to match whenever possible. They're always telling secrets, and they're always located right next to each other whenever they're together. I know, I know, it seems odd, but I'm an only child from a fucked-up family. Who am I to judge someone else's family dynamic?

The worst part about Lawrence would have to be his size. Oh, he's tall enough, five-foot-eleven. The size of his little friend, though, let's just say the rumors *aren't* true about the correlation from hand to dick size. He has big hands.

Don't get me wrong; I'm not discriminatory to dicks. I'm all about dick positivity and whatnot. The problem with Lawrence is he practically *only* uses his dick. Mouth, fingers, toys, all too much for him. Of course, I've tried to have the conversation and spice things up in the bedroom, but he'll just agree, try it once, and then never do it again. At that point, I'm too embarrassed to bring it up again.

I'm alright though. Thank God for my healthy imagination, the internet, and my faithful vibrator, Buzz, as I like to call it.

There are some good things about Lawrence. He's good-looking, in a Ralph Lauren kind of way. He can be judgey, but he did decide to pick me of all people. Well, most guys would pick me in a crowded room. I've got huge boobs, pornstar lips, and an ass that won't quit. But I'm also poor, come from a shitty family, have no friends, my humor is not for everyone, and I don't seem to know when to stop talking. I'm not everyone's cup of tea, but Lawrence picked me. I'm not entirely sure why, besides being smoking hot and hilarious, but I *am* thankful he did.

My life went from eating ramen noodles and wondering how I would pay off my useless student loans to vacationing in Bora Bora and picking out everyday china for my wedding registry.

It sounds shallow to say that money makes up for everything I don't like about Lawrence, but that's not the case. The sense of security, a future, the freedom that Lawrence gives me makes all the other bad parts about him a little... blurrier, and that's enough for me. It's more than I've ever had.

It's been almost an hour of this silent mind-fucking boringness, and I'm tired of being alone with my thoughts. I stand up.

Everyone stares at me as if waiting for an explanation I'm not supposed to give.

"I'm going to take a nap," I proclaim.

It's followed by shushes from the instructor and horrified looks from the rest of the girls.

"Oh yeah, silence. I forgot," I say over my shoulder as I walk out of the meditation hut. One of these women is definitely going to shank me tonight.

I'm ready to get my mind off of my own miserable life.

Besides, I got a hot date with Buzz.

CHAPTER TWO

Beck

No calls for help. No blood-curdling screams. I guess it's a shitty morning already. I peer into the hole of my trap just to be sure. Maybe I got a rabbit, at least. That would be somewhat of a snack.

To be fair to this morning, my human meals are few and far between. No one usually ventures out this far into the swamp, and that's how the community likes it.

The magical community is all about secrecy and keeping themselves hidden. They fear that if someone discovers talking wolves or gnomes, the government would be all over our shit. We have cable and internet, so we know what the real world is like. The running theory is that if they discovered us, they would either kill us all, practice science experiments on us until we want to kill ourselves, or the worst option of all... turn us into an attraction. If I ever have children lining up to take pictures with me, just know the end times are near.

Because of so much threatening our tiny community, they decided to put me at the entrance. Just as an extra safeguard. Right past all the "DO NOT PASS: PRIVATE PROPERTY. PERPETRATORS WILL BE SHOT ON SITE," signs. My rationale for trapping and eating them is that they clearly want to die. I mean, there's a sign, come on.

Although we only get about three stragglers a year, it always freaks the board members out. They're worried that families will start looking and discover us. Luckily, almost everyone who's disappeared in this swamp is a homeless junkie with no one to care. I recommended changing the signs to "DO NOT PASS: PRIVATE PROPERTY. PERPETRATORS WILL BE EATEN BY A OGRE," but the board members said this change would defeat the purpose. Idiots.

I do my best to make the human meat I do get last, but I technically don't need it to survive. I can live off deer, alligators, or the chickens I breed and keep. But nothing beats that smokey taste of human meat. All that fast food they eat really does something for them.

I'm the only ogre in my community. It can be rather lonely being the only seven-foot, green, hilarious, *and* gut-wrenchingly handsome creature around, but it's a cross I bear. I do enjoy not having to share my food, and for that perk, I'll take being alone any day.

I adjust the sticks and brush back over the opening of my trap. Here's to hoping tomorrow is a better day. I make my way over to my garden. Some people, at least from the fairytale books I've ordered on Amazon, think that ogres only eat meat, and that could not be further from the truth. Vegetables are one of my favorite food groups. In fact, my favorite meal is potato, carrot, and eyeball soup. Nothing beats it.

Gardening is also a great hobby for me. It keeps me busy, and there's something just so erotic about moving my fingers in such a way as to make sure each delicate seedling grows to its full potential. I like to work with my hands and find different ways that improve my dexterity.

I haven't always been alone. When I was young, I did have parents, but they didn't last long. As I find, most creatures don't. It's better to keep busy and find things that you enjoy than get entangled with someone that could leave you, betray you, or be stupid enough to die.

So, it's just me, my chickens, my vegetables, and the hopeful prospect of a human meal every morning. What more could an ogre ask for?

CHAPTER THREE

Liona

I wake up already out of breath. It feels like every one of my nerve endings is vibrating. I'm unsure of where I am and try to pull my arms down, but I can't. I look up at the metal headboard to see my wrists are tied. I'm naked. My body is oiled, and I'm lying on satin sheets.

I should be panicked. I should be wondering why the hell I'm exposed and bound in a place I don't recognize, but surprisingly all I feel is a sense of calm and wanting. I'm waiting for him. I know he's coming.

I struggle against the ropes around my wrists, ignoring the pain. In fact, enjoying the pain. I don't want to escape.

I want to touch myself. My cunt is throbbing, and it feels that if someone doesn't take care of her, I might explode. I writhe my legs together. The small friction between them gives me an ounce of relief, but it's not enough.

The sweet whine of the door opening makes me pant. I almost want to yell for him to hurry, but I stop myself.

The room is dark, only illuminated by candles at the far edge.

He walks slowly. His steps are loud and determined.

My pants grow heavier, desperate. Until he finally gets to the edge of the bed.

"I need you," I moan. My legs are still rubbing against themselves, and I pull against my bindings.

He chuckles. "Be a good girl and stay still." His voice is deep and gruff. Just the sound of it sends a shiver down my body.

He starts at my feet, licking me with a tongue that feels too large to be human. He works his way up until he's at my inner thigh.

"Yes, please," I moan.

But he stops. "You need to be quiet, or I'll tape your mouth. Is that what you want?"

I can't gather words to respond.

He goes back to licking, starting at the bottom of my stomach. He makes his way up slowly, his licks getting longer and deeper. His tongue rubs over my nipple, and I moan loudly.

"Do you like that?" He whispers into my ear.

"Yes, more." I open my eyes now that his face is by mine.

It's a familiar face. It's Lawrence.

I feel as if someone dropped a bucket of water on me. I look around, and the room is suddenly transformed. I'm not naked in satin sheets, bound by the candlelight. I'm in Lawrence's sterile gray and white room, wearing an oversized t-shirt and no bottoms. Lawrence is on top of me, already pumping away and nearly finished. His croaks speed up as he climaxes on my stomach.

I scream.

***

I wake up. For real this time. I'm sweating and panting, and not in a good way.

Who has nightmare sex dreams about their fiancé? Probably someone who should see a therapist, but it's not like I can talk to anyone about this, even if I wanted to. I'm at a silent retreat. Besides, not one of these girls would be my choice to discuss my confusing cold feet with. They would just tell me to stick it out because he's *so great*, which is code for *he's so rich, and you're so poor and hopeless.* They would be right, of course, and that's probably exactly what I need to hear right now. I'm just not in the mood.

I sit up and look around the room I'm sharing with my bridal party. All the girls are asleep in their matching PJ sets and facemasks. I'm surprised my scream didn't wake anyone up.

My heart races a hundred miles a minute, and I need to move. I can't even think about trying to fall back asleep. I grab a pen and a notepad from the bedside table next to me.

"Going to clear my head. Don't look for me." I scribble. Not that I think any of these girls would wake up from their slumber and go on a frantic goose hunt for me, but it's better to be safe than sorry.

I pull my windbreaker over my gray t-shirt and boy shorts and quietly lace up my boots on the floor. I grab my phone and wallet. Maybe I'll walk up the street to the nearest diner and get breakfast in the morning if I'm still not ready to deal with this silent retreat and my apparent besties.

Until then, I'll be taking a solo walk into the forest. What's the worst that can happen?

CHAPTER FOUR

Liona

I'm not trying to be a pick-me-girl by saying that walking alone in the woods at night doesn't scare me. In fact, there's not a lot that does. So my solo trek through these woods outside of the silent retreat is practically a cakewalk.

Growing up, we lived in a trailer in the middle of the Oregon woods. My parents would constantly forget me at school, the grocery store, my friend's house, you name it. I had to learn how to find my way back real quick, and I couldn't let anything as silly as night and an owl hoot freak me out.

The silent retreat has had some type of iron gate around the facility, blocking all cell phone and Wi-Fi service. I'm hoping that if I get far enough away, I can find some bars and distract myself with some mindless social media scrolling. I don't really know where I'm going. The retreat is deep within the woods, and I didn't feel like taking the dirt path that got us here. I've always been the one to go the road less traveled.

Even though I still can't find any service and I'm still alone with my thoughts, it does feel considerably better not to be around people I feel I must put on a show for. Even when they're sleeping, I can feel them judge me.

I should be used to it by now. The judging. Growing up, I was always the smelly kid. Not only were we poor, but my parents were also alcoholics, which, ultimately, was why we were poor. Being poor would be bearable but having your parents wrestling in the middle of your town Walmart on a Tuesday afternoon was a whole other type of embarrassment.

As usually comes with having alcoholic parents, the abuse came as well. They would hit me, pull my hair, put out their cigarettes on my freckles, the whole gamut. It's hard to find the strength to care if someone is judging you because you're wearing TJ Maxx leggings instead of Lululemon when your childhood was like a WWII battlefield. But, since I started stepping into this LA socialite lifestyle, the judgments *are* getting to me a little bit.

I know I have so much to be thankful for. I don't have to work, I live in a kick-ass apartment, and anything I want is mine with just a swipe of Lawrence's credit card that he so graciously bestowed upon me. All the romance books and movies would tell me that money can't buy happiness, or you can't settle for someone who doesn't set your panties on fire, but those sentiments aren't reserved for girls like me. They're reserved for people with parents to fall back on and an uncle that can get them a secretary job at their law firm. I have nothing and no one. I need to make myself fit into this lifestyle even if it evaporates my soul. Even if I'm subjected to mediocre sex for the rest of my life.

I've gotten so lost in my thoughts of my past and my reasoning for continuing with this marriage, that I realize I have no idea where I am. I make a 180-degree-turn to decide the best way to proceed, but it's pitch black; the only light comes from my almost-dead phone.

My heartbeat thumps louder. How could I be this stupid and let myself get this lost? I keep walking. There must be a road somewhere along here. My phone dies, and I'm surrounded by darkness.

As I said, I'm not afraid of being alone in the woods, but I'm much more high maintenance now than when I was eight. If I don't have coffee in the morning, I might actually pass away.

I start walking faster, thinking that if I can get *somewhere* faster, then I might be okay. Tree limbs smack my face, and every few steps, I trip on something in my path.

I take a second to breathe and collect myself. "Okay, Liona, think rationally. Look around and see where you are."

My eyes have adjusted to the darkness and the moon and stars overhead provide me with enough light to see a boulder to my right. I climb on top and stretch to my tippy toes. Just a few feet away, beyond the canopy of trees, is a billow of smoke. There must be someone who lives out here. I survey my route before climbing down the boulder, hope filling me.

I walk towards the path, hoping the house doesn't belong to a serial killer and is actually a 24-hour pancake factory.

As I walk along the path, I see a small cottage in the distance, illuminated by light streaming from the windows. It looks so quaint and inviting. Surely, it's just a little old grandma baking cookies. I pick up my step and charge towards it.

Suddenly the ground gives out from underneath me. I scream before I hit the floor, and everything goes black.

CHAPTER FIVE

Beck

I can't think of a better way to be awoken than from a human scream. It was just one scream followed by a thump, then silence. I hop out of my bed like a little kid on Christmas Day, at least how I've seen them on TV, grab my lantern, and run down the path leading to my trap.

I don't hear any sound, which probably means the drop knocked them out. Although I love eating humans, I'd rather not see them in pain and petrified. I hope the fall did the killing for me, honestly.

I hold the light over the hole. I'm frozen.

Lying at the bottom is a woman. Not just any woman; she's beautiful. She has jet-black hair lying over her tanned skin. Even from far away, I can see her lips are full and red, and her eyelashes are thick. She almost looks like a doll lying on the dirt floor. Her chest rises and falls, letting me know she's still alive.

I shake my head, wondering if the loneliness is catching up with me and I'm imagining her.

I've seen a human woman before, on TV and online, but never in real life, and never one this gorgeous. The only humans to drop into my trap have been old men. I'd never even thought about eating women or children, and thankfully I've never had any drop in my trap to leave me to figure out what to do with them.

The pit's large enough for me to hop in next to her. She's so tiny compared to me. I gather her unconscious body in my arms and then climb out.

In my arms, I get a chance to gather her features under the moonlight. Her skin is so peachy compared to my green skin. She has a trail of freckles down her nose that looks like a constellation of stars. She's covered in dirt from, I imagine, wandering through the woods and falling, but she still smells like fresh cotton. She wears a tattered grey t-shirt, and the outline of her nipples are like pearls I want to put my mouth on. Her skin is unbelievably soft, and with one hand, I wander from her neck to her collarbone to her breasts... I stop there, even though I want to explore more. I want to touch every part of her. I want to place my lips on her. I imagine her skin tastes like honey. It looks like honey. I don't want to eat it, just taste. Taste every part of her.

I bring my mouth closer to her neck, unwilling to stop myself, when suddenly, she stirs in my arms. The movement startles me, and I tense.

Her big blue eyes slowly blink open, and I wait in anticipation to see their full effect.

She finally focuses her attention on me. Her face immediately morphs from its peacefulness to absolute horror. She lets out an ear-piercing scream and begins flailing in my arms.

I'm snapped back to reality. I cover her mouth with my hand. She's so tiny that it covers most of her face. I look around to see if anyone heard or saw her. Shit. What am I going to do with her now that she saw me? I can't just leave her at the edge of the woods. She just saw me, an ogre. The secret of our community could get out. If the board members knew she was here, they would want me to kill her, and that's the last thing I want to do to her now. Tie her up and have my way with her? Absolutely yes. Kill her? Hell no.

I need time to think. I run back to my cottage with her in my arms like she's a sack of potatoes. She hits and kicks me, but she's so tiny and weak that it barely feels like anything.

When I get her inside, I place her on my bed. The minute my hand leaves her mouth, she screams like a goat. This is not going to work.

I pick her up like she's a baby, put my hand over her mouth again, and look around my cottage for something to put over her mouth.

She kicks me in the chest and scratches my arms. It doesn't hurt, though. Honestly, it just makes my dick even harder.

I grab cloth from the kitchen and tie her mouth and her arms. It's not easy. She is actually quite slippery and gets out of my grip a few times, but she's no match for me. In a matter of ten minutes, she's bound. My cock throbs looking at her like this, but then I notice her angry look has changed to a petrified one, and I immediately go flaccid.

I figure I should try to soothe her. "Hey, listen. I'm not going to hurt you, okay? But I need to keep you here until I figure out what to do with you."

She doesn't look calm. She gets up and tries to run towards the door.

I make one small step, catch her, and plop her back on the bed. I can't just tie her up. She'll keep trying to run away, and I'll be awake all night. I need my sleep so I can figure out what to do.

To the right of my bed is a giant cage. I don't always want to kill my meals right away. Fresh meat is better. Animal meat, that is.

I grab some pillows and blankets from my bed and try to make a bed for her on the cage floor. While I do this, she makes her way across the cottage and tries to unlock the door with her tied hands.

I chuckle. It's honestly so cute.

I lumber over and swoop her up again, place her in the cage and lock the door with a big brass key.

"Listen, I know you're freaked out. I'm a big scary ogre, and now I've kidnapped you and locked you in a cage. I know it doesn't look good, but I promise I'm not going to hurt you. We'll figure out what we can do in the morning, okay?"

She doesn't give me any indication that she's okay. I must have tied her gag tight enough because I can barely hear a sound from her. She wiggles and pulls at her bonds.

I sigh. "Alright, well, just try to get a good night's sleep. We'll have a big day ahead of us tomorrow."

I blow out the lantern and lie in bed. Of course, I don't fall asleep. How can I sleep knowing she's there next to me? Honestly, the cage was a good idea not only so she doesn't escape but also so it's less accessible to get to her in the night and do everything my dick tells me to. I've always been a gentleman. An ogre, but a gentleman, nonetheless. Tonight, I'll just defile her in my dreams.

CHAPTER SIX

Beck

"Order, order, I say!" Henry Coilsworth, our goblin board president, yells from the front of the conference room.

The emergency board meeting is in full chaos. Fairies flutter around, gossiping with each other. A giant pokes his head through the door, trying to listen in. The gnomes loudly chatter amongst each other at the front of the room.

"Silence!" Henry Coilsworth yells, breaking through the noise.

The room stills.

I rub at my temples, resting my elbows on my thighs. I'm ready for this mess to be over. I'm not usually the one to be the center of town drama, and it pains me to know I've caused such commotion.

Henry clears his throat and sits in the chair in front of the meeting room. "Obviously, we know why we're all here today, so I'll skip the formalities. Many of us heard the human woman scream last night and brought it to my attention first thing this morning. Beck has come forward and confirmed that a human woman *has* indeed stumbled onto our community."

The room bursts with chatter and angry questions.

Whenever a human comes onto my property, we always meet about it the next day to discuss just what happened in case there are any possible security breaches. It's never this rambunctious of a crowd. They must feel as unnerved as I am that it's a woman. If only they got a look at her, though, I bet many of the males in here would absolutely lose their minds.

The thought of any of them wanting to touch her makes my blood boil. She's mine. I found her. Even if she only stays with me for a little bit.

"Order, order!" Henry yells again. "We cannot keep behaving like animals!"

"Hey!" one of the bears yells.

"I apologize. It's a figure of speech. You know what I mean." Henry sighs. "Mr. Beck, please come to the front and discuss what happened with this woman so we can devise a plan."

I slowly rise. I've never been the most comfortable with talking to people in general. Speaking in front of a crowd? Absolutely shit-my-pants-worthy.

I stand up at the front and wait for the first question.

Henry begins. "Beck, how old does this woman look?"

I scratch at my head. "Uh, I'm not sure. Humans age differently than some creatures."

"Does she look like she's in her childbearing years?" he asks.

"Yes," I say dryly.

Murmurs pass through the crowd.

I know the reason he's asking me this. He doesn't have to explain. Just like me, it seems cruel to dispose of a young woman with so much potential. He hoped she was old and frail with only a few years left.

"And she definitely saw you?"

"Yes."

The crowd grumbles again, getting louder this time.

Henry clears his throat and pulls at his pointy ears.

The crowd silences again.

"Where is she now?"

"She's tied up and in a cage in my cottage."

"Good." Henry rubs at his green arms and sits up straight. He must have come to a decision.

"Well, there is only one logical thing we can do, no matter how hard it will be. You'll need to dispose of her. I imagine you won't mind. She'll probably make a tasty meal for you. Is there anyone who disagrees with this verdict?" He looks to the crowd.

They murmur in agreement.

"No!" I don't realize what I'm yelling until it's too late.
The crowd silences and looks at me.

"No?" Henry questions. "Beck, you know what a human witnessing one of us could mean. There's no way to return her to her civilization without her telling people or wanting to know more. I don't think I need to remind you what happened twenty years ago."

He's talking about my mother, of course. My pulse heightens that he would mention something I obviously know well.

"Don't tell me you're getting soft on us, Beck. You can't let the fragility of the human form cloud your judgment." He examines me closely.

I think quickly. "No, of course not. It just gets lonely and tiresome alone in my cottage."

Henry chuckles. "Well, I know one of the sirens would be happy to give you a visit."

I am not interested in the slimy and patronizing ways of the sirens. They live in the lake in the town center and transform their tails into legs whenever they make a house call. They only cost a chicken or two for their time with you, but I've never been interested in paying for companionship. No matter how lonely I get.

"No, I'd like to keep her as my prisoner. I need help with household chores and gardening. I'll make sure she doesn't escape. She is so slow and weak I could trap her with my eyes closed."

Henry rests his angular chin on his palm and taps at his temple, staring at me, seeming to see if I am really going soft.

I steel myself, hoping he can't see how I'm truly feeling about the woman. I don't just want her company; I want to protect her for some odd reason. It must be her rack. A nice pair of tits always ruins a man's judgment. But even I can't lie to myself. Watching her sleeping this morning before I left, the slope of her nose, the way her chest rose and fell as she breathed, it did something to me, and not just in my pants. I know there's something more.

"Very well," Henry finally says. "If you want to keep this woman as your prisoner, then I see no problem with that, but I must warn you, if this goes sorely, your head will be on the line."

I nod in agreement.

"Alright, this meeting is adjourned. The human woman will live with Beck as his slave."

Slave? I don't know if I like the sound of that.

***

"Aw man, come on! Just let me see her!" Donny tries to match my pace as I make my way back to my cottage.

"No! I'm not going to get her to do anything for me if I frighten her to death. It's probably traumatizing enough to be captured by a seven-foot-tall ogre. If I introduce her to a centaur on the first day, her heart might stop."

"Ah, shut up, man. Her panties are probably soaking just thinking about you. You know all the women in the village want you. She's probably just pretending to be scared of you, and she would be even happier to see me." Donny chuckles and smooths down his hair.

Some would say that Donny is my only friend because he's the only one I mildly converse with, but they would be wrong. I have no friends. Donny annoys the fuck out of me.

"Human women do not like big green ogres with fangs or someone who's half-man, half-horse. Fuck off, Donny."

"Come on, man, you're no fun! You got yourself a little plaything. Why don't you let me join in on the fun? That's what friends are for, right?" He smiles and pats his chest.

In one swift movement, I grab Donny by the throat and hold him up in the air. "Donny, I don't know how many times I have to tell you, but we are not friends. Stay away from me and stay away from my prisoner, or it will be your eyeballs I'm munching on for my next meal. Touch her and die." I throw him to the ground.

Donny rubs at his throat and regains his breath.

I keep walking. I've never felt this feeling before. Why do I want to burn down a city just at someone mentioning touching her? This must be what jealousy feels like, and

I don't like it. I can't let myself get too attached to this woman. She's my prisoner, and it can't be anything more.

"You're a dick, you know that man?" Donny yells from several paces behind me.

I flick him off without turning around.

CHAPTER SEVEN

Liona

At first, I wake up thinking I'm experiencing sleep paralysis. I can't move my arms or legs, but then I remember where I am. Honestly, I'm surprised I even woke up. I for sure thought I would find myself hanging over a fire like a roasted pig. I shouldn't be counting my lucky stars anytime soon, though. I know there are a lot worse fates for me.

The front door slams shut. I roll over to see the ogre that kidnapped me entering the cottage. How did he leave without me hearing him? Was I really that deep in sleep that I didn't notice? Talk about some shitty survival skills.

The only reason I know he's an *ogre* is because he told me. I've heard of ogres before in fairy tales, but he doesn't look like what I had grown up hearing about. Oh, he's definitely terrifying but different. The most alarming part about him is that he exists. Ogres are supposed to be fictional characters. I'm still not ruling out that I actually passed out in those woods, and I'm imagining everything. But then I feel the friction of my bonds and know this has to be real.

Another alarming feature about him is his height. I'm pretty short, five-foot-two, so everyone is tall compared to me, but I swear he's at least seven feet. He also has two large fangs almost touching his nose, green skin, and muscles on every inch of his body. If he wanted to, he could crush my skull without breaking a sweat, and that was proven to me last night by all my pathetic attempts to escape.

The most confusing part about him is why he hasn't killed me yet. I remember hearing that ogres eat people. I don't know what to believe, but looking at him, he could definitely devour me. Maybe he's trying to fatten me up?

Maybe he wants to play with his food? Whatever the reason is, it can't be a good one. He has a giant cage in his room, for crying out loud! There will definitely be some Dahmer shit going on soon unless I have a plan.

The ogre gives me a look as he comes in and then turns down his head. He seems almost shy or embarrassed. I can't be sure though; ogre facial expressions could be different.

I sit up and stare at him. I'm surprised at myself for how composed I'm behaving. Sure, there's no use in screaming or crying, I'm tied up and in a cage, but you'd think my little lizard brain wouldn't care. I should be screaming bloody murder until I pass out. I guess I do have some survival instincts left in me. It makes sense since I've had to survive my whole life. I guess my cushy, socialite lifestyle over the past two years hasn't sucked it all out of me yet.

Last night, the ogre said he wasn't going to hurt me. Of course, at that moment, I didn't believe a word he said and was on the brink of a panic attack, but now, watching him tip-toe around his kitchen making something, I wonder if he could be persuaded to let me go. I'm thankful he speaks English and not some unknown ogre language. Maybe we could talk this out. I must have some shred of hope.

I calmly sit in my cage and wait. Sweet smells start to drift over, and my stomach rumbles.

After twenty minutes, the ogre stomps over to my cage with a large plate in hand. He's wearing a tight cotton shirt and burlap-looking shorts. The clothes don't do much to hide what's underneath. He's bulging with muscles every-where. It honestly looks cumbersome to get around with so much mass. I know from experience though; he gets around pretty easily.

He sits on the edge of his bed, parallel to me.

I can now see that on the plate is what looks like French Toast.

Ogres can make French Toast?

I look around the small cottage. His bed is like a giant, circular bean bag; there's a small stove in the kitchen, a table with two chairs around it, cabinets, and other stor-age. Everything about his house seems surprisingly human. More Amish or Little House on the Prairie, but human. I wonder if this is all part of his ruse: make his victims feel comfortable, fatten them up and then roast them over the fire for the whole ogre village. *Oh, God, I hope there's not an ogre village.*

The ogre clears his voice. "Are you hungry?" He waits for a response.

I just stare and shake my shoulders in a "are you stupid?" kind of way.

"Oh, right. The gag. Here, lean close to the bars, and I'll pull it down for you."

I don't move for a moment. The thought of getting closer is terrifying, but I know I have to talk to him if I'm ever going to find a way out. I do as he says.

His fingers are *huge.* He grazes them on my cheeks and slowly pulls down the cloth tied around my mouth. His eyes are focused on mine. His breath is heavy and slow.

Oh my God, is he trying to have a moment with me? What a freaking idiot!

I must admit that his touch is warm, and he does smell surprisingly good up close. I didn't notice it yesterday. The whole being taken as a prisoner is pretty distracting. But if he thinks that he can woo me? He has another thing coming.

The moment the gag drags past my chin, I scurry to the back of the cage away from him.

He's knocked out of his trance and slinks back to the bed.

"Let me go!" I yell. It's a stupid demand. As if he'll be like, "you know what, that's a good idea. I'll just open your cage, and you can be on your way," but it's the only thing I want to say.

He sighs. "Why don't you just eat, and then we can talk?"

"Will talking lead to you letting me go?"

"Well, no, but..."

"Then no! I don't want to talk to you. I want you to let me out. What do you want from me? I have money. I could get my fiancé to pay you." It's a stupid offer, I know. What is an ogre going to do with money? But it's the only offer I have. Well, that and sexual favors, and I'm not desperate enough yet to start handing those out.

"You're engaged?" He looks wounded.

I can't help it. I laugh. "Yes. Why do you look so sad? Were you considering proposing?"

His brow furrows, and his nostrils flare.

Yep, he's definitely a terrifying ogre, and I should remember that before poking fun at him. I cower and hide my face with my arms.

I peek out at him from behind my hands.

His face is back to its neutral expression. In fact, his eyes look a little... sorry?

"You don't need to be afraid of me. I'm not going to hurt you." He sighs. "Let me untie your hands, and then you can eat."

I oblige because what else am I going to do?

"If you're not going to hurt me, what are you going to do with me?" I ask as he's focused on untying the cloth around my wrists.

He sits up and gives me eye contact again. His eyes are a golden hazel. "I'm just going to keep you here. That's it."

"That's it?" This answer almost seems worse than saying I'm going to be his sex slave. "Why do you just want me to *be* here? I have a life to get back to. I need to go home."

"Why were you wandering around the woods at night by yourself?"

I raise my voice. "Are you trying to do some sort of slut-shaming type shit for why I fell into your trap? I'm allowed to walk in the woods. I don't deserve to be kidnapped because I was walking in the woods!"

"Actually, you're *not* allowed to walk in the woods. There are signs everywhere about how this is private property, and trespassers will be shot. Were you trying to get shot?"

I make an offended gasp. "No! I didn't see any signs. It was dark! And if that's the case, why didn't you just shoot me?"

"Would you rather me do that?" He seems calm. Serious.

I shudder. "No. I'd rather you just let me go. Fine me or some shit, but don't keep me as your prisoner for no reason."

He places the steaming plate next to him and rubs at his temples. "I can't do that. It's too late. You have to stay here."

"Like fuck, I do!" I yell. "You can't keep me here. I'll just escape." So much for talking him into letting me go.

He laughs. "Honey, I'd like to see you try. I can smell you from a mile away. I can take one step and outrun you. You don't even know how to get through these woods. I suggest you *don't* try running away. You'll regret that."

"Well, I'm going to make your life a living hell until you let me go!"

He leans into the cage with a shit-eating grin.

I lean in too, with a clenched jaw. I want him to see I'm not going to back down. I'll be his worst nightmare.

His eyes go to my lips, and he licks his. "I'll just keep you tied in this cage, then." He shoves the plate of French

Toast under the bottom of the cage and stomps out of the cottage, slamming the door behind him.

"Ahh!" I scream at him as he leaves. I hate that fuck-face! I want to stab his stupid little grin and rip out his eyes.

I plop back on the cage floor, defeated.

The waft of sweet vanilla hits my nose. I probably shouldn't eat it. It could be poisoned. But my stomach is rumbling uncontrollably. I pick up one of the sticky pieces of toast and take a bite out of it. It melts in my mouth. Flavors of cinnamon, sugar, and maple flood my senses. I give a slight groan of pleasure. I'm glad he's left. I don't want to give him the satisfaction.

I sit there, munching on my breakfast and staring at a blank wood wall beyond the bars of my cage. I'm not giving up. I'm not going to let him just fatten me up with orgasmic French Toast and be his little pet. I'm getting out of here. I may not have the strength or agility to escape, but I do have one thing I think he's interested in. I saw the way he looked at me. He couldn't keep his eyes off my lips or my tits. I've used my body to get my way before. Heck, I would say I'm even doing it now with my upcoming marriage. I think the feminist gods will forgive me if I use a little seduction to get out of the clutches of an ogre.

Fuck that guy.

Operation Pussy-Trap, commence.

CHAPTER EIGHT

Beck

The door slams behind me and I trudge toward the fire pit. I pick up one of the stumps and throw it at a tree, splitting it in half. I'm not angry at the woman, mostly myself, and these stupid community rules. What did I think was going to happen? She would be so thankful that I didn't eat her that she would be my happy little worker girl and suck my cock every night after dinner? How could I be so stupid? This is never going to work.

When she said that she would make my life hell, I knew she was truthful. Although I've loved having her close to me, tied up and gagged, it's already been torture. Especially when she's angry. Ugh, when she yelled at me... it took everything in me not to break those bars and rip off the remains of her measly clothes.

The thing is, I could do that. I could keep her tied up and stick my dick into any of her holes I please. But I don't want to. Sex wasn't ever a topic on my mind in my solitude. It wasn't until I saw her lying on the floor of my trap that it all changed. Although I want it hard and rough, the thought of doing something she doesn't want makes me soft. I want her to beg for it. I want her to moan my name as I'm deep inside of her.

I sit on one of the remaining logs by the firepit and rest my head in my hands. Maybe if I can find a way to explain this to her, she would be thankful. She would see that I have no other choice but to keep her safe with me. Maybe I could even make her fall in love with me for being her hero. She doesn't seem like the type of girl to swoon over such basic decencies, such as *not* eating her, but maybe my good buddy Stockholm will help me out. It will make both of our lives easier, and I don't have any other options. The community would kill me *and* her if they found out I let her go.

I have to find a way to make this work. She doesn't have to love me or fuck me. She just has to stay alive and not want to murder me. That's it. I need to find a way to make that happen.

The first step: make her a delicious meal.

***

I come back to the cottage a few hours later. In my hands is a platter of roasted chicken, potatoes, and carrots that I made over the fire. I place it on the table and walk over to her cage.

The woman is lying on her side, staring at me. Her finger lazily drags across one of the blankets on the floor, forming an imaginary circle. She looks so relaxed, not at all how I would expect her.

"That smells delicious," she says as she licks her full lips.

I'm hoping my shorts do a good enough job of hiding my erection, but I know they probably don't; my dick's a hard one to hide.

As if reading my mind, her eyes trail down. She licks her lips again.

My heart pounds in my chest. I clear my throat and try to regain my train of thought. "I made you lunch. I thought we could talk while we eat."

"Do I have to eat in here?" She stands up and presses herself against the bars, giving me a pouty look. Her dark brown hair in silky waves falls over her shoulders and her breasts seep through the bars. Her nipples are hard, and her thin gray shirt seems even thinner.

As if she notices me looking at them, she pulls herself away from the bars a bit and grabs her breast. "I'd love to come out and get to know you better." Her voice is low and sultry.

Her other hand travels down to her shorts. She plays at the waistband with her finger and then dives in. The outline of her hand moves up and down as she plays with herself.

I can barely take the sight. My knees are weak, and my dick is as hard as a rock. I long to stroke it.

In the back of my mind, I know what she's doing. A few hours ago, she promised to make my life a living hell. There's no way she just suddenly decided she wants to fuck me, or at least let me watch her fuck herself. It angers me that she thinks of me as so weak. I most definitely am, but I don't have to let her know that. I know she's trying to escape, but what if I played along?

I move over to the bed parallel to her cage, sit down with my legs spread, and pull out my cock from the top of my waistband.

Her eyes grow wide. "Whoa, you're big." The tone of her voice seems genuine and surprised, but I know she's probably just saying that to butter me up, even though I know it's huge. I've seen other creatures' dicks around town in the springs. Mine is the biggest by far.

There are already drops of pre cum at the top, and I rub my hand over to lubricate my stroke.

Her eyes focus on my motions and droop into slits; her mouth opens in a moan. "Why don't you open up the cage and let me suck you dry?"

I know what she's trying to do. Although she is a very convincing actress, with her hitched breathing, the expression on her face, and the sound of her fingers gliding up and down her wet pussy, I'm not falling for it. "Nah, I'd rather watch you." I begin to stroke faster.

At first, she looks disappointed, her brows furrowing, but then she purses her lips and reaches for the hem of her shirt, pulling it overhead.

I didn't think it was possible to get any harder, but seeing her perfect bare tits makes my hips writhe from my seat. I moan at the sight of them.

She circles her taut nipple with her finger. They're pink and match the color of her pouty lips.

My mouth waters as I imagine her finger as my tongue. I bet they taste fucking fantastic.

Her other hand is still down her pants, sliding up and down. She must be wet. I can smell her sweet, aroused scent.

How is she faking this? While in town, I've heard fairies murmur about "faking it" with their lovers. They laugh as if it's a common thing among women, but how can she be so convincing? Maybe she's not faking it....The thought makes my balls clench, begging to burst, but I slow my stroke, wanting to last longer than she does.

She closes her eyes, her breath getting heavier and her moans rising to a higher pitch. Her skin is spotted with goosebumps.

I have to stop rubbing my dick entirely. Just the sight of her pleasing herself makes me have to hold back my seed.

Her moan turns to a yelp, the cords in her neck straining, her fingers working wildly. She's coming undone and I make sure to commit her movements to memory. I want to be the one to make her scream like this. I want to be deep in her wet fold as she yells my name. But right now, I just want to watch.

Her body slacks and her hands stop their movements.

I stay seated, lounging on my forearms with my manhood still proudly standing tall.

She slowly opens her eyes, sobering up from her pleasure. Her cheeks blush as if embarrassed. She looks at me as if waiting for my reply.

This pleases me. I won. There's no way she faked that. Although my balls are swollen and begging to come all over her full chest, I restrain myself. At least for now.

I carefully place my hard cock back into my shorts and struggle to stand up. "Ah, well, that was a fun show. I bet you worked up an appetite there. Ready to eat?" Trying to play nonchalant.

Her cheeks are no longer a blush pink but an angry red. Her full brows furrow over her ocean blue eyes. She quickly pulls her shirt back over her head and straightens out her clothing. "Are you sure you don't want me to make you come all over my face?" Although I can tell she's still trying to keep up her act, I can hear the anger at the back of her throat. My dick still throbs at her words though.

"I'm good for right now. I just want to eat." I fish in my pocket and pull out the brass key. "Why don't you sit at the table with me?"

Her eyes grow wide in shock, and I can't help my grin. I open the door and motion for her to exit.

"Aren't you afraid I'll escape?" She looks puzzled as she walks out onto the wood flooring.

"Of course not. You try to escape; it will be a matter of minutes before I've got your arms tied behind your back and you sprawled across my bed." I laugh.

She doesn't.

"You're a dick," she growls before plopping in one of the seats at the table.

"Oh, I love it when you talk dirty to me." I sit across from her and chuckle. So far, my wooing isn't going well, but if she wants to play games, I'll join in. Besides, this is so much more fun.

CHAPTER NINE

Liona

I would have thought it was impossible to hate the ogre sitting across from me anymore after he kidnapped me and locked me in a cage. But here I am, not even twenty-four hours later, hating him more than the devil himself. Capturing me, eating me, that's understandable. He's a monster; it's in their nature. But keeping me as his prisoner so I can just sit around, then making a fool out of me while I came all over myself and he watched, well, that's just... I don't know... worse than a monster.

It wasn't in my plan to orgasm. Well, I meant to fake one at the most. I've faked orgasms for the last two years; I'm pretty much a pro at it. I know he wants me. I saw how he salivated over my tits and how hard his cock was. He stroked it with so much restraint, as if he moved any faster, he would burst. I know I shouldn't have liked that. He's a monster, for God's sake, not even human, but I can't deny he is handsome in a smug, annoying kind of way. I knew his dick would be big. He's seven feet tall and built like a boulder, but God... seeing that thing... imagining it deep inside me... I couldn't help myself. I haven't come like that in years. Now, I'm thinking back on it and can feel my wetness against my thighs as I sit at the table with this monster and try to focus on my hate, which I need if I ever plan on getting out of here, and I do.

We've been eating in silence for the last five minutes. I'm so embarrassed and angry I have nothing to say, and he just seems so pleased with himself. *The bastard.*

He clears his throat. "So, what's your name?"

The question surprises me, but then I realize I just fucked myself to a guy whose name I don't even know. I don't want to give him any more of myself, even my name, although I can't help wondering what it would sound like coming from his lips.

"Liona," I say, surprisingly sweet.

"Liona," he says in his gruff voice.

I can't help the pang between my legs at the sound of it.

"I'm Beck. Nice to meet you." He offers me his hand. His hand that's the size of my face.

My heartbeat pounds as I think of his giant fingers grabbing me, feeling me between my legs. Oh my God, Liona, get a hold of yourself! This is Operation Pussy-Trap, not Operation Stockholm Syndrome!

I still can come out victorious in this. Yeah, I might want to fuck him, so what? I can still hate someone I want to fuck. I do not want to be a prisoner here. I want to be back at my stupid little silent retreat with all my vapid bridesmaids, even though I don't even have hope any of them will come looking for me. I want to be Mrs. Farque, flying privately to Bora Bora and eating unlimited caviar. I can still get out of this. I just have to continue playing the game. A little slip up doesn't mean I've lost.

I flash a smile and grab his hand. "Nice to meet you, Beck." I pull my hand back and giggle. *God, I'm good.*

Beck's face scrunches up in skepticism.

Maybe I'm not as good as I thought. I think he can see through my bullshit.

"So." I relax my face and twirl a strand of my hair around my finger. "Tell me, why do you want me to stay here with you?" I lick my lips and then bite one of the chicken legs on my plate. A slight moan escapes my lips. *God, he's a good cook.*

Beck stares for a second and then shakes his head a bit as if lost in his thoughts. "It's not that I want you to stay here with me."

I can't help the drop of disappointment in my stomach. "Oh no?"

"I'm not the only creature that lives around here."

Oh God, the ogre village...

"There's a whole village of magical creatures that live in a community. Fairies, gnomes, centaurs, elves; the whole fairytale crew."

"Are you fucking with me?" This is hard for me to believe. Sure, he's an ogre, and there's no doubt about that, but this just seems... comical.

As if reading my thoughts, he says, "No, I'm not. I'm the only ogre though."

Thank God for that.

"I live at the edge of the community to protect it from visitors. The trap that you fell into, that's for any human that wanders too far."

"Well, I don't see a whole slew of humans running around your cottage, so am I the first one?"

He turns down his gaze. "No."

"Oh... so..."

"You're the first woman, though. I could never hurt a woman or children," he says defensively.

Maybe I should be more frightened of him than I am. I've imagined he's eaten humans before, but to hear him imply it... it scares the shit out of me.

He babbles on. "I don't think I could eat another human again."

Ah, don't say that. Fuck, why did my mind go to a dirty place?

"Why?" I ask.

"I've met you, and now it seems wrong."

"I would agree. Very glad you decided not to eat me." I look down at my bare plate. "Besides, this chicken tasted fantastic. I don't see why you would need to eat anything else."

"Thanks." He blushes, and honestly, it's kind of endearing

What's wrong with me?! This guy just told me he ate people, and now I think he's endearing.

"Why can't you just let us go?"

"Because then our community wouldn't stay hidden."

"So? People would love fairytale shit."

He stretches his arms over his head and runs his fingers through his shoulder-length brown hair. His bicep flexes as he does. "Yeah, history hasn't been very kind to us."

"Like when? I've never even heard that ogres or any of those other creatures are real before."

His face sobers. "We've done a good job at making sure news doesn't get out widespread, but there have been some small slip ups." His eyes seem sad.

I decide now is not a good time to press more. I'm trying to get him to like me. Even though he explained why he has to keep me, I still don't want to stay here. I appreciate he didn't eat me, but I still want my freedom.

"What if I promise I won't tell anyone? Can't you trust me and let me go?

"It's too late for that. The community knows you're here, and they barely allowed me to keep you alive. If they found out I let you go, they would kill you and me."

"Aren't you the big, scary ogre? How can they threaten you?" My voice shakes.

"There are about two hundred creatures in our community. Some of them are great warriors, magical wizards, and even giants. They could get me. I'm just the guy that volunteered to guard the border. I like my solitude."

"Oh." I look down at my hands resting on the oak table, trying to hold back tears. Now what? Now I'm not just trying to escape an ogre; it's a whole army of scary beasts.

A tear slips down my cheek.

"Hey." Beck reaches out and grabs my hand. "It won't be that bad. I think you might like it here if you give it a chance. I'll give you a tour of the property today. There's a spring nearby, a garden, and other... cool stuff." He smiles.

I know he's trying to be sweet and helpful and protect my life, but right now, he's just annoying. He's an obstacle in the way of my freedom. I want to lash out, to tell him to go fuck himself, but he's the only person I have on my side right now. I know he said that if he let me free that the community would kill me, but I have to believe there's a way out. I can't give up yet.

I still need to escape, and Operation Pussy-Trap is still a go. I will get out of here, even if I die trying.

I brush away a tear and smile up at him. "Okay, sounds fun."

CHAPTER TEN

Liona

My lug of an ogre dragged me all around his never-ending property. Our first stop was the much-needed outhouse, which I cried in for fifteen minutes.

Beck kept knocking on the door, making sure I was okay.

I just couldn't get over the fact that I might spend the rest of my pathetic life shitting in a hole outside. Sure, I'd grown up roughing it, but I'm used to the finer things at this point in my life. Lawrence has a God damn bidet. I can't say I actually miss *him* right now, but I sure as hell miss his toilet.

I needed to put on a brave face. I *will not* be shitting in a hole for the rest of my life. I am getting out of here.

Beck is a man of few words, which after the days at the silent retreat, I'm thankful for. If he turned out to be a talker, it would probably shock my system. Well, on top of the already intense amount of system shocking.

He showed me the spring a few hundred feet away from the cottage. It's crystal blue and seems to have no bottom. Probably a great place to drop the remains of a body. Unless he ate the bones, I'm not sure, and I have no intention of finding out.

He showed me the chicken coop, the garden, and various trees around the property that grow fruits. After three hours, I was pretty sure he was just trying to wear me out so I wouldn't try to run away. Although he successfully made me tired, I still planned to execute my escape tonight. Even though I probably wouldn't make it, I had to try.

The sun is nearly completely hidden behind the canopy of trees when we return to his cottage. Beck goes straight to the fireplace to heat up the room. Although we're in Florida, it's January, so tonight feels chilly.

"Do you want anything to eat?" he asks while poking at the fire.

I sit at the edge of his bed, rubbing my aching feet. It sure took a lot to keep up with a seven-foot monster, even though I could tell he was trying to slow down for me. "No, I'm just tired." I'm honestly not hungry after the two over-the-top meals Beck served me. I'm probably the only kidnapping victim in existence to be so royally stuffed.

"Alright, you can go to bed. I'm just going to make something for myself real quick."

"Do I have to sleep in the cage tonight?" My plan of escaping hinges on him saying no.

He stops what he's doing and looks at me. "No, but I only have one bed, so you will have to sleep with me." I swear he says this while looking at my tits.

"Can't you be a gentleman and sleep on the floor or something? It's the least you can do after kidnapping me." It's going to be harder to get around him if we're sharing a bed, but not impossible.

"No, thanks. If you want to sleep on the floor, you can."

"Dick," I whisper to myself.

"Oh, I'm sorry did you want something? It sounds like you've got one of my body parts on your mind." He gazes at the fire with a snarky grin.

I flop over to the head of the bed and pull myself under the covers, grumbling angry nonsense to myself. *It's fine*, I think. *I just have to pretend to fall asleep for a few hours, and then I will never have to be in the same room as him again.* At least, hopefully. Very unlikely, but hopefully.

Beck's plan works though. After only ten minutes, I'm unable to keep myself awake. I drift to sleep.

***

It's dark when my eyes shoot open. I don't know what could have woken me; all I hear is the buzz of frogs in the swamp and soft breathing. My eyes adjust to the darkness and focus on the figure beside me.

It's Beck, lying on his side, facing me. I've never been this close to him, and although the only light I have is the moon shining through the window behind him, I finally get to make out more of his features.

I've known he's entirely muscle, but now I can see just how much of him there is. His head barely touches the pillow since his giant arm he's resting on lifts him so high off the bed. It doesn't look comfortable, having to move around with so much mass. Although, personally, I'd love to see just what his body could do to me. He could break my neck without even exerting much energy, and for some odd reason, that turns me on. *God, do I need a therapist.*

He's still threatening in his sleep—his fangs touching his cheeks, his jawline so sharp they could cut a diamond—but he's still objectively handsome. I never imagined ogres could be good-looking. They're supposed to be horribly ugly, but I don't even think it's my apparent Stockholm Syndrome speaking when I say how hot he is.

He could definitely be on the cover of GQ Magazine. It would be a strange edition, but it would sell millions.

My eyes travel down his chiseled body. He doesn't have any covers over him, which makes it easy for me to take in every part of him. I'm not sure if I'm relieved or disappointed to discover he's wearing pants, but not just any pants, no, gray sweatpants. Are you shitting me? They have gray sweatpants in his secluded wilderness village?

My bafflement is almost immediately covered by gratitude because the gray sweatpants do their job alright, revealing the outline of his glorious cock. I'm delighted to find that he's hard. I wonder what he's dreaming of. I can't help but hope he's thinking of me touching myself in his cage. Or maybe of him ramming his massive dick inside of me. I'm not sure I'd be able to take it. It looks too big for any human, but I can't say that the thought of trying to fit it in doesn't thrill me.

Yes, once I get out of here, immediately going to therapy.

Before I even know what I'm doing, my hands are down my pants. I might as well get myself off before I try to escape. It'll help me stay focused. I'm so unbelievably wet. I didn't even know I could get this wet. As I watch my sleeping ogre, my fingers slide up and down with ease until I focus on circling my clit. I imagine his arms around me as he pumps into me, and I feel myself about to come, but I want this to last a little longer. I close my eyes, knowing that looking at his perfect form is too much if I want to hold out. I imagine his tongue licking me from the inside out.

I'm near the edge of my climax when I hear a slight moan. I open my eyes and gasp. Beck is awake, biting his lip. His dick is outside of his gray pants, and he's rubbing it slowly.

I pull my hand out of my shorts, embarrassed, even if the sight of him stroking his cock to me makes my skin prick. He caught me. I don't want him to know what he does to me, but it seems as if he's gotten the better of me yet again.

Before I can move or say anything, his gruff voice breaks the silence. "Can I help?"

If only I would have orgasmed, then I could think clearly, but right now, my pussy is purring. I want him so bad. How can I say no?

"Yes." It's more of a moan than a word.

In a flash, Beck has removed the space between us, his completely solid body now pressing against me. His dick throbs at my belly. It's harder than it looks, and I resist the urge to grab it. I feel drops of wetness trail along my belly as he slowly and lightly grinds against me. He moans as if he's already inside of me. His arms hold on to me like he's holding on for life. He feels for my breast. I've always thought I was well-endowed with my D-cups, but feeling his massive hand around them makes me feel small.

"Beck," I whisper softly as he lazily feels one of my nipples.

"Ah, fuck. My name's never sounded so good." His voice seems pained, like he's close to the edge. His fingers trail from my nipple down to my side. He slowly drags it lower and lower until he brushes the inside of my thigh.

"I want to hear you yell my name," he whispers before he pushes me flat on my back and dips his giant finger in me. "God, you're so wet."

I feel his dick pulsing at my side.

I've never orgasmed from just penetration before, but Beck's finger is bigger than Lawrence's dick. He nearly fills me with just one. I'm close to the edge, about to come undone from just one finger inside of me, but then Beck pulls it out and rubs up and down my pussy. He hits my clit at the top, and I moan with pleasure.

"I tried to remember your movements when you were touching yourself in my cage. I noticed this is the spot that made you crazy," he whispers in my ear as he circles my clit. "I want you to moan my name." He demands.

That's it for me. My body tenses, and I feel a million waves of pleasure rush over me. "Beck!" I yell because it's the least I can do for the guy. Plus, it's the only thing I want on my lips. Except his dick. I want it so deep down my throat and in my pussy that it touches the other side.

My orgasm lasts for a few more seconds, and I twitch as I come down from it. Beck's finger slows as I do. Once he stills and my body relaxes, I realize the gravity of my situation. *Fuck. What the fuck did I just let happen?*

I immediately flip to my side, away from Beck. I know it's a dick move. The guy just gave me the best orgasm of my life, and I didn't finish him off or even say thanks, but this never should have happened. Sure, I wanted it. Bad. And sure, it felt fan-fucking-tastic, but I *am* running away tonight. This ogre kidnapped me. It would be one thing if I fucked him to distract him, but that's not what's going on.

Beck stays still for a few moments.

I anticipate him rolling me over and having his way with me. I don't want that, but at the same time, *God,* I want that. He's an ogre, a monster, and I felt how hard his cock was. He wants me, and he's probably about to ensure he has me. But then, to my surprise, he rolls over and scoots toward the other edge of the bed without a word.

I'm shocked. I've never been with a guy that performed sexual favors and then didn't expect anything in return. They were human men, not even seven-foot-beasts, that could do as they wished without any repercussions. I don't get it, but mostly, I'm disappointed. A part of me, the stupid part, wanted him to take me, but I know this is good. This is what needs to happen because I can't fuck him. I have to get out of here.

This time, I'm not falling asleep. I'll wait until he dozes off, and then I'm out. Horny or not.

CHAPTER ELEVEN

Beck

I'm an idiot, the biggest idiot to ever live. Sure, her fingers were deep in her folds, watching me. Sure, she was so wet my entire dick would have slid into her seamlessly, and she even said "yes" to my request to take over pleasuring her. But I should have known it was too soon. She hates me now.

I've never been with a woman. I've been alone my whole life and happy that way. Sure, I've jerked myself off at the thought of the feminine form before, but that's nothing like the real thing. There's an instinctual part of me that knows what I should do, where I should touch, where I should taste, especially with Liona; she was made for me. But so far, every time I think I know what she wants, I'm wrong.

My cock begs to release as I lay on my side, facing away from her. It took everything in me not to burst just from having my finger deep inside her. And when she yelled my name... God damn it, I've never had to exert so much strength.

I'm a monster, but I need to start behaving more like a gentleman regardless of what my primal instinct tells me to do. And right about now, my body screams for me to roll over, grab Liona's waist, pull down her cotton shorts, and thrust my cock so deep inside of her that her pretty little lips moan my name until she's unconscious from the pleasure. But she pulled away.

That mortified look on her face when her climax settled over her will be one that's hard to forget. She was ashamed of herself. I could see that, and I'm the bastard that made her feel that way.

I would never forgive myself if I let my urges take control and had my way with her. The thought of hurting her or doing something she doesn't want pains me. I'm not sure why she has such an effect on me. This is the type of danger I've always been afraid of. I feel as if I would die for this woman I barely know. But I do know her. She's mine. I feel it deep in my core. The second I saw her lying at the bottom of my trap, I knew she was made for me and me alone. My instinct tells me to mark her, to fill her with my seed, but I want to make her want it. Not just in the way she clearly wanted me when she woke me up from my dreams. I want her to want me so deep within her that she begs for me. I have to make her want me.

Tomorrow, I vow to myself that I will seriously start my journey of wooing her. Although it's been fun to tease her and watch her try to resist her primal urges, the games are over. The teasing is getting too heavy to bear, and I don't think my dick can take it anymore. Tomorrow I will start making her want me as much as I want her. It might take a while, *God I'm going to have to find somewhere private to jerk off if it takes too long,* but it will be worth it. I want her to be happy here.

Tonight will be a long night. The stiffness in my cock doesn't seem to be letting up. I close my eyes, imagining Liona sliding up and down my cock. That will have to be enough to get me through. At least in my dreams, I can fuck her. I let myself doze off.

CHAPTER TWELVE

Liona

I kept my promise to myself. I didn't fall asleep.

Although I'm facing the wall opposite to the window, I can tell it's getting lighter outside. The dark oranges pool in, making shadows on the wall in front of me. It's nearly morning and I hope Beck is asleep heavy enough for me to leave without him noticing.

I slowly sit up and look over to see if he moved.

He's still.

I peel the covers off of me, watching him the whole time, and place my feet on the floor. My heartbeat is pounding as I tip-toe across the room to the door. My hand is on the doorknob when I freeze, catching one last glimpse of him. I feel a pull toward this sleeping ogre. Looking at him still has an effect on me, even after my orgasm. I was hoping that would settle the euphoria I feel toward him. I imagine it's because he didn't fully take me. A part of me regrets turning away from him last night. Now I will never know what it feels like to have him inside of me. It's probably for the best though. If I feel this attached to him now, I can't imagine what I would feel like if we had sex.

I've had casual sex before without feelings getting in the way, but standing here, on the brink of my escape, watching Beck sleep, I know it would be different. Maybe it's the Stockholm Syndrome, maybe it's something else, but I'm not sticking around to find out.

I make it to the other side of the door, closing it gingerly. If Beck were to wake up and find me now, I could just say I had to use the restroom. I take a few barefoot steps before sprinting toward the woods without any direction. I just need to get away, as far as I can from this place. I know this isn't a good plan, but it's the only one I've got.

In the early morning glow, the woods look much different than when I wandered through here at night. Nothing looks familiar, just a wash of gray moss and pine trees. My lungs burn and I try to ignore the searing pain every time I step on a branch or a rock with my bare feet.

A part of me hopes he catches me. It's crazy. I wonder if it has to do with the fact that I don't love Lawrence and I'm just looking for an excuse to get out of this marriage, but I can't decipher it, and I don't want to think too much about it. I just need to focus on getting away.

As if he heard my silent wish, loud crashes come from behind me, like a freight train barreling through the forest. I turn around and see Beck in the distance, shirtless and barefoot, swinging through trees and jumping over obstacles in his path.

Panic fills me and I ignore my aches, using everything in me to propel myself faster. Even in this fear, I feel a wanting. I know he won't hurt me, but I wonder just what he'll do when he catches me. The thought thrills me in a strange, animalistic way. I don't slow down though. A mixture of fear and intrigue storms inside of me.

It only takes a few more seconds until he's right behind me. His hand reaches for my arm. I try to pull away, but it's no use. My strength is nothing compared to his. I stumble, falling to the ground on my front.

Beck falls on top of me, using his hands and knees to support his weight so he doesn't crush me.

The adrenaline is still pumping in my veins and I dig my fingers into the dirt, trying to crawl away.

Beck grabs my hips from underneath him and flips me around to my back. His hazel eyes seem darker. His nose flares with his labored breaths.

"Get off of me! Let me go!" I yell, pounding my fists against his unmovable chest.

In one swoop, Beck grabs both of my wrists with one hand and pins them to the ground above my head. I scream. I know even if anyone can hear me, no one will come, but for some reason, knowing this excites me. It almost feels like a game, like I knew my attempts to escape would end up like this; me lying on the floor, sweaty and dirty, with Beck's pulsing muscles hovering over me, ready to devour me. It all reminds me of my dream, before it turned into a nightmare, the night I decided to wander through the woods. Maybe this is destiny.

"Let me go!" I yell again, gritting my teeth at Beck's unreadable expression.

With his free hand, Beck grazes from my head down to my waist. His eyes study mine.

My breath hitches, but I don't make a sound. I don't want to scare him away.

My cotton shorts are nearly shreds of fabric at this point, making it easy for Beck to gently graze over me and find his way between my legs.

I'm unable to suppress my moan, even though I still want to keep up this game.

His hand remains still over my entrance.

I suppress the need to grind against him.

Slowly, he brings his lips to my ear. His breath sends goosebumps down my skin. "If you really want to escape, why are you so wet right now?"

Any reserve left in me dissipates. I bite my lip and close my eyes.

His finger wiggles just slightly, gently entering me.

"Beck," I moan.

He grazes his fangs against my neck and then returns to my ear. "You have two options. I can either let you go, or you can let me spread your legs open and lick your pussy until you're begging me to fuck you."

I freeze. Like that's even a question? "Fuck you!" I get out angrily before turning my head and pressing my mouth to his. I mean it. I'm angry at him for his effect on me, but I also mean that I want to fuck him.

I'm unsure if he's kissed anyone before because, first, he seems shocked. But then I work my tongue between his lips, and he seems to get the idea, matching my movements and kissing me back as if he's starving.

Our kissing only lasts a few minutes as I writhe from the ground and against his hold on my hands, trying to get more of him.

He quickly moves down to my waist and rips what remains of my shorts. I'm not wearing underwear, but right now, I wish I was. I wish I were wearing an endless amount of clothes so that I could watch him tear them apart in desperation.

He lays on the ground beneath me, holding up his body with his elbows. He pulls my legs into the air and begins trailing his giant tongue from the middle of the inside of my thigh to the entrance to my core. His tongue is rough and probably the size of my hand.

"Beck, I need you," I yell when he stops there. I feel as if I might die if I don't have him between my legs. I'm dizzy with pleasure just from the anticipation.

"That's a good girl. Open up for me," he says in a husky voice before trailing his tongue between my folds. He starts slowly, moving up and down starting from my entrance.

When he gets to my clit, I almost come undone immediately.

"Fuck!" I yell.

"Ah, I knew that's where you liked it."

I appreciate his pause, so I don't come so quickly. It's never been this good.

"When you come, I want to hear you scream my name. I want all the nature around us and everyone in a hundred-mile radius to know you're mine. You taste like mine."

He starts again, licking faster. He circles my entrance, poking his tongue in and out of me. He slides up and down a few more times and then focuses in on my clit, circling in perfect rotations.

"Beck!" I yell in a moan of ecstasy. I reach down and hold on to his biceps as the wave passes through me. Every nerve ending seems to be electrified and my body feels weightless.

He keeps going. Devouring me as if it's his last meal.

When my body unclenches, Beck crawls up from my legs to my ear. "I know I said I'd never eat a human again, but you taste so good. I'll eat your pussy for breakfast, lunch, and dinner." His fangs gently bite my earlobe.

Although my orgasm just passed, the need to come again floods my body. "Fuck me, Beck. I need your cock inside of me."

CHAPTER THIRTEEN

Beck

Her words send vibrations through my body, and my cock aches. A primal instinct in me urges to thrust so deep inside of her and fill her with my seed. Licking her was better than any meal I'd ever tasted, but I realized just how tight she is. I don't know if she can take me. One thing is for certain, if I don't stick my dick somewhere inside her soon, I might die.

Her grey shirt is as flimsy as her shorts and I rip it in half, exposing her full breasts. Her nipples are taut and just the sight of them makes me want to come all over her chest. But I know that won't do. I'll never be satisfied until I have her sweet pussy gripping me, pulsing as she comes. I want this to last.

So instead, I suck on her nipples and reach for her cunt, still soaking wet with her delicious honey. I thrust one finger inside. She moans with pleasure and a shiver runs down my spine. I thrust my finger in and out. As I do, she opens more for me, allowing me to stick another finger inside.

"Beck, I need you. Now," she sobs.

I want to take longer but her words make it impossible. I pull my cock out of my sweatpants and position the head at her entrance.

"I don't know if I can take you," she whimpers.

"You will. You were made for me." I ease in the tip and her sobs echo through the forest. She opens up for me like a flower in full bloom. Her cunt makes way as I stroke in my full length, starting off slow.

"Beck. Fuck me like you hate me!" She grabs my neck and pulls me up to her, her lips capturing mine again.

I take that as permission to increase my speed and she moans in my mouth to the rhythm. Her fingers are yanking at my hair and I try to pull away from her face just enough so I can watch her come undone.

"Scream my name for me, baby."

"Beck!" she yells as her pussy pulses and her body writhes and bucks.

"Fuck," I yell as I climax inside of her, filling her up. I pump in a few more times until my body feels like mush. I lie next to her and look down to see my seed overflowing from her. It's a puddle beneath her.

We lay there for a moment. I watch as the early morning sun shines from the canopy of leaves overhead. The only sound is our content breaths and the birds chirping in the distance. I've never felt so full. I'm completely empty, but it feels like I have found my purpose. Making Liona come is all I want to do for the rest of my days.

"I don't think I'm going to be able to walk back," Liona says, breaking the silence.

I sit up. "Did I hurt you?" I look over her body, glistening with sweat but dirty. She doesn't appear to have any injuries.

She searches my face and then brings up her hand and cups my chin. "No. I'll just be sore. I've never been impaled by a monster dick before. It was top-notch, but yeah, I'm going to be sore."

Without hesitation, I swoop her up in my arms. She gives a little yelp in surprise. Her body is tense at first but then, after a few steps back toward the cottage, she melts into my arms, rubbing her cheek against my chest.

I swing the door open and place Liona on the bed. Her eyes are droopy and she curls up against one of the pillows. I can't help feeling nervous about how exhausted she is. I know she said I didn't hurt her, but I don't like seeing her weak. Even if just a few moments ago, I wanted to fuck her brains out.

I rush to the fire and start boiling water. I need to clean her. I'm ashamed of how dirty I let her get.

By the time I've got the water, soap, and towels ready, Liona is passed out. I start washing her face, wiping away the dirt, and once she's clean, it's like seeing her for the first time. Her skin is a soft golden hue with freckles lining her nose. Her cheeks are rosy and her lips look like a plump rose. She's like a doll. My perfect personal plaything, but she's so much more than that.

Her eyes flutter open while I clean her but she seems to be so exhausted that she lets me proceed without much movement. When I get to her breast, I notice her nipples are hard again and my dick grows hard at the sight of them. Her skin flushes with goosebumps. She's as aroused as I am, but I know she needs rest. When I get to her cunt, my hands tremble. I can barely focus on cleaning her and do my best to resist the urge to bury my face into her sweet folds. She gives me a moan. I know she would be ready to take me again, but if she's sore now, she would be practically broken if we did it again this soon.

I grab some oil from one of the cupboards and begin to massage her legs, working close to her inner thighs. I want to heal her, to make her good as new. I can't wait long to bury my cock into her again, but making her feel good this way will have to do.

"That feels good." She opens her eyes and looks down at me. Her lips are parted and her breath is heavy.

"Please don't run away from me again. I can't protect you if you leave," I say as I work my hands up her body.

I lie next to her, cradling her in my arms.

She gives me a sober look. I'm not sure if I'm reading her right, but she seems to understand. She can't leave. *She's mine.*

CHAPTER FOURTEEN

Liona

When I wake, I'm not sure if I'm still in a dream. I feel more rested than I have in ages, and there's a euphoric feeling running through my veins. I'm warm and comfy and snuggling up to a massive figure. When I look over, I remember where I am, and when I try to sit up slightly and feel the soreness between my legs, I remember what I did.

I feel like I should be embarrassed or pissed off at myself. I just fucked my captor. But I don't feel bad about it. In fact, I feel better than I have in a long time.

I turn on my side to face Beck and run my hand along his angular jaw.

He stirs and grins. "I thought I would be awoken from hearing your footsteps snapping twigs through the forest again."

"Well, I thought I would wait until tomorrow to run away." I look down and nuzzle against his pecs. They're so warm, and even though they're not soft, they're cozy.

"Ah, well, I guess you're going to have to run away naked. Your clothes are ripped to shreds."

"You'd like that wouldn't you?" I wrap my legs around his middle, feeling his erection harden at my words.

"It would make it less work for me when I catch you again and fuck you against a tree."

"Okay, now you're just encouraging me." My hands are already reaching down his pants, grasping his hard cock. I can't believe this thing fit inside of me.

He gives an airy sigh but then pulls away. "Wait." He looks pained. "We probably should go to the village and get you some new clothes. All the shops close in a few hours. As much as I would love you walking around naked, I don't think I'd get much done that way. I need to feed you."

How about you feed me this dick, I want to say, but I think better of it. He's right. *God, I would kill for some underwear.* Besides, the thought of seeing the village excites me. I don't know if I've fully accepted that I'm staying here with Beck, but I'm more comfortable with the idea and want to see my potential new neighborhood. Maybe I'm going crazy, but after having sex with Beck... staying doesn't sound too bad.

I flop to my back and sigh, already sexually frustrated after just a few hours. "Well, what am I going to wear into town?"

Beck sits up and ties his unruly shoulder-length hair into a top-knot. "I think I have a potato sack around here I can cut some holes in."

"No! That can't be my first impression! They probably already think I'm your sex slave."

"Aren't you?" he asks in a mocking tone while he steps into his pants on the floor. His ass is two perfect round boulders.

I pick up my pillow and chuck it at him. "You dick!"

He turns around, a giddy grin on his face, and then pounces on top of me.

I can't help but giggle. It's surprising how comfortable the two of us have become in just a few hours. To think, just last night, I was contemplating my escape. Now I'm giggling and rustling around in the covers with him. I guess that's what good dick can do to you.

"There you go talking about my dick again," he whispers in my ear before kissing down my neck.

"What, is your sex slave supposed to be quiet and polite? What are you going to do if I'm bad?"

A fire blazes behind Beck's eyes. He grabs my hands and holds them over my head. He returns to my ear and whispers, "Bad girls, get tied up and fucked until they plead for me to stop."

I moan and throw my head to the side. "If that's the case, then you're in for a world of trouble. I'll never be good." I try to wrap my legs around him and pull him into me.

"I wouldn't expect anything else," he says before he presses his lips against mine.

Our kissing becomes more passionate, and I struggle against his grip but he doesn't let me go. Finally, he pulls away and walks over to throw on his shirt.

"Wha... what are you doing?" I sit up and gawk at him.

"I told you. We need to go into town."

"But...can't we just go tomorrow?" All the cool girl reserve in me is gone. I'm desperate.

He smiles at me. "Ah, so now you know how it feels. Do you know how hard it was for me not to fuck you when I first found you?"

"This is very different. I'm conscious. You're conscious and both of us are willing individuals." I'm bargaining. I'm fucking bargaining for sex.

He walks over to me, buttoning the top of his shirt. "We both know you wanted me the minute you saw me."

"I did not!" I lie back down with my arms over my chest.

Beck laughs and then begins rummaging around the kitchen. I assume getting my sack dress ready.

"Can't you just go to the town without me? Just pick something out you think I would like." Even though I was excited to see the town, I rather not look like a house elf when I could potentially meet a real life house elf.

"I'm not leaving you here alone."

"Why?" I snap up. "Do you think I'll run away?"

Beck busies himself with the burlap fabric and scissors, but I can tell he's grasping for the right words. "I'm not sure. I just can't protect you if you're not with me."

"Protect me from what?"

"Well, mostly yourself. If you do try to run away, then you could be killed."

"What do you think I'm doing now? Pretending to like you so I can get away?"

"I mean, it's not like you haven't done it before." He looks over at me defeated.

I get up and walk toward him, ignoring the soreness between my legs. "I'm not faking. I wanted you. I still want you." I step in between him and the counter and wrap my arms around him.

It takes him a few moments, but he eventually hugs me back. "So, you're happy to stay here with me then?"

With my head pressed against his chest, I say, "Well, I don't know about that. I'm not going to try to run away but maybe we can figure out how I can get back home, together."

He pulls me back. "No, Liona! There's no you going back. If we tried to get you back, they would kill you and me. I've seen what they can do."

I put my hand to his chest and can feel his heartbeat racing. "Okay, okay," I say, because I can tell he's genuinely frightened. I put my head back on his chest.

I don't know if this is what I want, but right now, it doesn't seem like I have any other choice. Maybe I can figure something out Beck hasn't thought of, but for right now, I guess I'll just be an ogre's sex slave. The thought genuinely thrills me.

CHAPTER FIFTEEN

Beck

I'm not usually one to appreciate the simple beauties of my everyday life, but walking through the town square with Liona gives me a new set of eyes. She looks around in wonder at the shops and creatures around her. She's still gorgeous, even in her potato sack dress that she laughed at for fifteen minutes, tears falling down her cheeks and crouched over. Everyone gawks at her as we pass, and she looks at me, rolls her eyes, but smiles as if everyone thinks she looks ridiculous. But really, I can tell, everyone is taken by her. A fire burns deep in my stomach and I hold onto Liona's hand.

She smiles at me as if this is a sweet gesture, but really I just need everyone to know she's mine. And her touch calms me. I would need nothing else in life, just to touch her all day.

When we come to a bend, I see Donny in the distance, standing in front of the pub. He waves at us and then looks Liona up and down, licking his lips. Blood rushes to my head and I'm about to break off in a sprint and strangle him, but my thoughts are interrupted by one of Liona's questions.

"Who is that?" Liona whispers to me every few seconds as we pass a new creature. She doesn't seem frightened by any of them, even the Chupacabra with his rows of fangs proudly displayed. I tell myself this is because she's with me. She must know nothing can hurt her while I'm by her side.

"How does this all stay hidden?" she asks in awe.

"As you can probably tell, we're serious about keeping it a secret. We've had strong relationships with local government for a long time. They keep us a secret and we make it worth their while."

"How?"

"Some of our members are pretty valuable. For example, we have an alchemist."

She nods and looks around, taking everything in.

We finally arrive at the Clothing Shoppe, a cream-colored cottage with flowers in boxes at the windows. When we push the door open, a bell rings from the top of the door and lets Gilda, the Fairy Godmother, and owner of the store, know we've arrived.

"Wow, it's beautiful!" Liona exclaims as she reaches for a green dress embroidered with pink flowers.

"Well, hello there!" Gilda floats out of the back room, fabrics draped over her shoulder. "You must be the human everyone's talking about." She flitters around Liona and examines a lock of her hair. "I can see why Beck has taken a liking to you. Although, I think we could do better in the fashion department. Is this what you came to our village in?"

Liona laughs nervously. "No. The pajamas I showed up in are shredded."

Gilda gives me a knowing look. "I wonder how that happened." She turns back to Liona, a smile on her wrinkle-strewn face. "No bother, dear. Let's get you into the back. I'll whip you up some clothing that fits you like a glove." She leads Liona back and I step forward to follow. "No, no, no. You can stay out here and wait. It'll be a surprise."

Panic encases me, and my heartbeat pounds in my chest.

Liona touches my arm lightly. "It's okay. I'll be right back."

My fear melts a bit. "Okay," I try to say calmly but it comes out more strained than I would prefer.

I take a seat at a bench by the window, pressing my palms together in an effort to suppress my nerves. I shoot up when the bell chimes, and someone enters the store.

"Beck, how you doing, buddy?"

I stand up and peer over the corner to see Winston LaRue. Winston is a kind and reserved fellow. He's one of the youngest wizards in the village and he's without a long white beard and flowing robes. He's muscular and tall and likes to wear more modern clothes. I wouldn't say we're friends. We only ever talk at town meetings, but he is tolerable enough.

"Hi, Winston. I'm fine." I give a pained grin and sit back down.

Liona yelps from the back room, and I burst back up, ready to charge. When I hear her and Gilda giggle, I unclench my fists and breathe out.

Winston chuckles. "I see you're here with the lady, huh?"

"Yes." I look at him, my jaw clenched.

Winston strides closer to me and whispers. "I'm glad I caught you here. I've been meaning to talk to you about something since the town meeting the other day."

"Hmm," I snort, barely paying attention to him.

"I could tell you care for this human."

My focus snaps to his words at the mention of *my* human. *My* Liona. "Yes."

Winston gives me a wide-eyed look, like he can sense my aggression at the surface. "It's just, I wanted to let you know that I have a potion to wipe her memory. I know none of the old-timers are going to mention it to you. I guess we all kind of thought you just liked eating humans, and that's why you had your job, but I wanted to let you know there's another way."

"What?" My stomach drops. I grab Winston by his collar and raise him in the air.

He yelps, and fear is in his wide eyes. "If you wanted to let the woman go, you could just give her the potion and she would forget everything she saw here."

"Does anyone else know about this potion?" I snarl.

"The wizards do, but they don't really care about the humans. They would never mention it."

"Good." I put him down and pat his shoulders. "I want you to keep the news about this between the two of us. Got it?"

"Yeah, yeah, of course. No problem, man." He laughs nervously. "I just wanted you to know, just in case."

"Why don't you get out of here?" I open the door and motion for him to walk through.

"But my pants... you know what... I'll get them another time. Good seeing you..."

I slam the door behind him and watch him jumpily walk down the street.

"Did someone drop by?" Gilda asks as she flies out from the back.

"Oh, it was just some kids..." I attempt to explain more but stop once I see Liona emerge.

She's wearing a white flowy dress with sleeves that fall off her shoulders. Pieces of her hair frame her face but most of it is up in a delicate arrangement. Her waist is cinched, and even though the skirt hangs loosely, I can see her curves. It's like she was chiseled from marble. She's too perfect for words and that's why when I try to say something, I come up short. My mouth just hangs open as I examine every inch of her.

Liona smiles as she walks towards me.

"Well, what do you think?" Gilda asks, clearly very proud of herself.

When Liona gets close enough, I pull her into me, crouching down to her ear. "I think that I would take you here if I weren't so worried all the townspeople looking in would want to partake as well."

"Beck!" she yells in a whisper before turning to Gilda. "He said he liked it." She looks to me and shakes her head.

"I knew he would. Now I have a few more skirts, blouses, and pants for you in a bag at the front." She snaps her fingers and it appears at the register. "Let me get you on your way. It seems you two will be rather busy the rest of the day." She winks before flying toward the back.

Liona hits me. "You need to cut it out! She definitely thinks I'm your sex slave."

"What? You didn't mention how much you loved riding my dick this morning?" I whisper, but probably a little too loud.

"Shut up!" she whispers, but smirks. "Can you just chill until we get back home? I'm trying to make a good impression."

Home. I know she probably didn't mean it, but it sounds so good coming from her lips. Winston's revelation wrestles around in my head, but seeing her so beautiful and hearing her admit to my cottage as her home... I can't tell her. She's mine. She has to stay with me.

CHAPTER SIXTEEN

Liona

I've never imagined that I would enjoy the slow lifestyle. I've spent so much of my adult life struggling in LA, and then once I wasn't struggling anymore, I was going from event to event every day. The busyness of my life never allowed me to be alone with my thoughts, which I enjoyed. Since my short time at the silent retreat and now living in the desolate cottage with Beck, I've had a lot of time to think. In fact, probably too much time.

I've tried to keep myself busy with gardening, journaling, taking long walks, and, oh, sex. Yes, lots and lots of sex. I used to think that I would be happy if I could get off a few times a week. Now it feels like if I don't have some part of Beck's body inside of me every few hours, I *will* die.

We don't *just* have sex, to be fair. We've spent a lot of time together doing house chores, playing little games, and talking. Beck seems to have as much childhood trauma as me, maybe even more. He won't reveal all of it, but it sounds like he grew up most of his life all alone. Both of his parents died when he was young and the reason seems like a touchy subject.

I've never been so intimate with someone. I definitely wasn't this close with Lawrence. I spent so much time telling myself that passion and intimacy weren't necessary for a good life or a good marriage. Now I'm not so sure. This is why being alone in my thoughts is so terrifying. What if I actually like my life here? And what if I actually have *real* feelings for Beck?

Today, Beck has decided it's time to cut a whole city's worth of wood. I spend a good hour watching him as he throws an axe over his head, his muscles tensing, and then brings it down to cut the log in half. It's so hot; I seriously almost have to start touching myself so I can think clearly. I probably could demand that he take a break and fuck me, but I'm already pretty sore from this morning's session. My body needs a few more hours.

I inform Beck that I'll be taking a dip in the spring. He swears that it's safe to swim in and although I'm usually terrified of secluded bodies of water, what else is there to do?

When I get to the spring, I pull my casual knit dress over my head and place it on a rock. Beck said that although people in the town know of the spring, no one ever visits. Hopefully, a leech won't crawl into my vagina.

I dive in, letting the coolness burn my senses until I finally get used to it. I try not to focus on how deep the water is and float on my back, staring up at the cloudless blue sky. Peace settles over me and I think the only thing missing at this moment is my ogre.

A rustle comes from the woods at the edge of the clearing. Beck must have heard my silent wish and has come to claim me in his pool. It's his mission to defile me on every inch of his property.

"I was wondering if you'd come find me." I'm smiling, sitting at the edge, waiting for Beck to appear from the brush.

Except, it isn't Beck who emerges.

"Ah, just the person I'd hope to find alone someday." Out walks a creature who has the torso of a man and the lower half of a horse. A Centaur. I've seen them in movies and storybooks but never imagined they could be real. He has long curly blonde hair, piercing blue eyes, and is without a shirt, revealing a muscular torso. The horse half of him is brown with a blonde tail.

I scream. Not because he's frightening, but because I'm naked. I cover my chest and sink deeper into the water, hoping it can provide me some covering, even though the water is so clear, I'm sure everything shows.

He chuckles. "No need to be afraid. I'm not going to hurt you. I'm a friend of Beck's."

This doesn't calm me. "Okay, cool dude, but I'm naked right now. Can you leave?"

"Relax. In this community we're very comfortable with nakedness. Hey, I'm not wearing any clothes right now either."

"That doesn't make me feel any more comfortable." I gave him a death stare, floating towards the center.

He shakes his head. "You're right. I'm sorry. I've started on the wrong hoof." He scoops down and picks up my dress from the rock. "Why don't you come on out and get changed? I bet you'd like some company besides the ogre." He smiles a pearly white grin and offers me my dress.

Great, now the guy is holding my only way out of being naked. I slowly swim over to the edge, watching him cautiously. I snatch the dress out of his hand and run behind a shrub, yanking my clothing overhead.

The centaur laughs. "So, what's your name? You're quite a mystery around town."

"Liona," I call from behind my brush. "Yours?"

"I'm Donny. I'm surprised Beck hasn't mentioned me. I'm his one and only friend."

"Yeah, he's never said anything about you before." I walk closer to him while wringing out my hair.

Donny's eyes trail down my body, and I suddenly feel naked again. He scoffs. "Figures; he's so secretive about things."

"Yeah, I know, he is." I feel a little guilty about agreeing with Donny. I'm not sure why.

"Ever since both of his parents died, he's been a recluse. Did he tell you how it happened?" Donny removes the distance between us and lounges against a fallen tree trunk, tucking his horse legs underneath him.

I feel inclined to sit next to him. Although I have a bad feeling about this guy, I can't resist the urge to know more. "No, he didn't tell me how they died, just that they did when he was young."

"Oh, man, it's a rough story." He rests his head on his hand. "Well, we used to be not so concerned about our privacy. Beck's parents lived on the edge but not necessarily to protect us. One day a young boy stumbled past the signs and the gates. Beck's mom felt bad for the kid and tried to help him find his way back home. I guess the kid's dad wasn't too far behind and shot Beck's mom. Beck's dad heard the commotion and ran out to find his wife with her head blown off." He chuckles a bit, which is creepy. "His dad killed the boy's dad, but after a few days, he was so depressed about his wife, he took the very same gun that killed her and shot himself in his own head. Beck was the one who found him."

"Oh my God, that's horrible." Tears are welling in the corner of my eyes. No wonder Beck has always stayed alone. No wonder this community is so afraid of humans.

Donny waves his hand as if dismissing the thought. "Yeah, but I guess ogres are more conditioned to deal with that kind of stuff. They're always killing and torturing."

"I thought that you said you guys were best friends. It doesn't seem like you know him very well." I lean back, starting to realize my initial intuition about this guy is right.

He laughs a deep belly laugh and then wipes the corner of his eyes. "Aw, that's so cute. Your Stockholm Syndrome has already developed only after a week."

"You don't know anything about me, or Beck, for that matter!" I yell and start to stand up, but before I can, Donny grabs my arm.

He pulls me toward him. "How about I show you what it feels like to be with a real magical being instead of that smelly ogre?"

"Let go of me!" I yell, and Donny covers my mouth with his other hand.

"Wow, you are a handful. No wonder Beck wanted to keep you to himself." He removes his hand and smashes his lips against mine.

I keep my mouth clenched, but every part of him is strong. His tongue inches into my mouth. I struggle under his grip, but he moves me against the fallen tree trunk. His horse body is still seated, but his human torso is pressed against me. His hands start to wander, one reaching for my breast while the other travels under my dress.

There's a small moment of release of pressure from his mouth, and I turn my head to the side and scream as loud as I can. Donny's hand darts to my mouth, and his other reaches for his giant penis, stretching from his horse half.

Not even a minute later, I hear Beck's thunderous steps running through the forest.

Donny looks up and releases me. I scramble from under him just as Beck swings through the clearing, only taking a second to assess the scene, and then charges at Donny.

Beck grabs Donny by the neck and slams him toward the ground.

"Hey, man, chill! I was just playing around. You shouldn't be the only one to have all the fun with the community prisoner."

Beck smashes his fist into Donny's face. Blood spurts from his nose. "Liona is mine," he repeats after each punch across Donny's jaw.

At first, I just watch, honestly overjoyed that this prick is getting the beating he deserves, but then I notice the amount of blood splashing on Beck's face and think I should intervene. Although I don't mind seeing the guy dead, I feel like it might have some consequences we wouldn't want to deal with.

"Beck!" I yell, but Beck's proclamation to ownership over me is too loud. I get closer. "Beck!"

This time he whips around, blood covering his entire front side. His eyes are dark and crazed.

"I think that's good." I lean over to see Donny's face bloodied and mangled, but his chest rises and falls. He's still alive.

Beck steadies his breath, looking down at Donny.

I touch his arm, and his other swings over and grabs me. "Did he hurt you? Where did he touch you? Fuck! I should kill him. I can't stand the fact that someone else touched you." He hovers over me, and I back up, leading us away from Donny's unconscious body.

"It's okay, I'm fine, really. You came just in time." I try to soothe, but it doesn't seem to be working.

"You're mine. You were made for me. How could he not see that!" He pulls at my dress and starts ripping it from the middle. "You're mine. Only mine."

He wants to claim me, I can see it in his eyes. He's going to devour me.

He grabs my exposed body and holds me in his arms, bringing me up to his face. I kiss his lips, tasting the blood of another man, a man that tried to defile me, and electricity runs through my veins.

Beck can hardly control himself; he's kissing me as if he's starved. He finally comes up for air, gets to his knees, and lays me on the ground, only feet away from Donny's battered and unconscious body.

"I fucking hope that prick can hear when I fuck you, and you're screaming my name." He rips his shorts off, revealing his manhood, hard as stone.

I never knew seeing someone covered in someone else's blood could turn me on so much. I want him to impale me and I'm already wet enough to take him. "Take me. I'm yours!" I moan, but Beck grabs my legs and throws them over his shoulders. His face meets my core, and his tongue licks up and down. He comes up for a breath. "You taste like mine!" he moans and then buries his face back into me, swirling his tongue up and down, and then focuses in on my clit. It only takes a few seconds before my body is clenching, my nerves sputtering off with pleasure.

When my body stills, Beck looms over me. His face is still painted in blood, except for around his mouth. "I want you to let him know how much you want me. Tell the whole world that your cunt was made for me." He orders me and then sticks in one of his fingers. "You're already ready for me. Good girl." He positions his cock at my entrance and thrusts into me without hesitating, with a need to claim me.

He's not taking his time. He pounds me hard.

"You."

Thrust.

"Are."

Thrust.

"Mine."

Thrust.

He repeats over and over.

I feel myself coming undone again. "I'm yours, Beck!" I yell, as loud as I can.

Beck pulses inside of me, filling me. His thrusts become slower, and he leans over to my ear. "I love you."

Oh, fuck.

CHAPTER SEVENTEEN

Beck

Liona doesn't say anything after my unexpected confession of love. I was caught up in the moment. I didn't mean to say it, but once it passed my lips, I knew it was true.

I lay next to her for a few moments, catching my breath. The reality of the situation sobering me. I turn over to check Liona, "Are you okay?"

Her eyes are closed and she's covered in blood. I'm hoping it's Donny's, but the sight panics me. I lean over and examine her.

"I'm fine. It's not the first time I've had some creep try to cop a feel. Usually, his balls are closer to my knee height, but luckily you were here." She turns to me and smiles, but I can tell there's concern behind her eyes.

"But did I hurt you?"

"Beck, don't worry about being too rough with me. As you said, 'I was made for you.' I can handle it."

She sits up and looks over at Donny's body. "Do you think he's dead?"

Honestly, I couldn't care less if he lives or dies, but it would be annoying to have to explain myself to the community. I get up and examine him, checking his vitals and his breathing. "He'll live. I won't be doing anything extra to ensure that, though," I call to Liona.

She nods before standing and walking into the spring.

I follow after her and help wash the blood and grime off her silky skin. She returns the favor, rubbing her hands over my face, my shoulders, and below my waist. Her touch arouses me again and I hold her close, grinding up against her.

She leans in, meeting my lips. Her legs wrap around my waist. She grabs my sex and positions it at the entrance of her sweet cunt. She pulls herself onto me, moaning softly.

I'll be gentle with her this time. The rage and need to claim her have settled now. I just want to be close to her. Although she didn't say she loves me back, this act shows me I didn't scare her away. She still wants to be near me, riding me, moaning my name.

I hold her breast with one hand, and with the other, I lean her back in the water, thrusting into her as her top half floats on the surface.

She comes first, her pussy pulsing around me. The sight of it sends me spiraling after, and I hold her close to me.

We sway in the water for a few moments, until I realize how tired Liona is. I lay her in the water, my hands under her to support her while she floats. The sun shines on her face, giving her an angelic glow. Her chocolate hair swirls around her and all I can do is stare in wonder. I do love her. So much. Not just because she's beautiful or because her cunt feels like heaven on earth. I love her humor, her sarcasm, and her ability to face life head-on. She's everything I'm not and so much more.

I like to forget that she told me she was engaged. We've never brought up the topic again. I don't know if she just told me that so I would let her go, or if she really has someone back home waiting for her. It wouldn't be that hard to believe. How could someone like her not have someone?

I wonder if she loves him. I wonder if it's possible to love two people at once. I don't know if she loves me but there's something in how she looks at me that makes me believe it's possible.

Liona is mine. I feel it in my veins, in everything in me. But loving someone and claiming ownership over them is not the same. Now that I know that the love I feel for her is more than I could imagine, I need to think about what's best for her.

I haven't forgotten what Winston told me about the potion. The more I fall in love with her, the more the guilt settles in. Liona doesn't have to live here with me. How can I know if she ever loves me if I don't give her the choice to not? But more importantly, how can I keep someone I love from the life she want for herself? This place isn't for Liona. Donny's a prick but I doubt he's the only creature that would think less of Liona and that they have dominion over her. I don't want the members of this community to think of her as my property. Property can be stolen or damaged with a slap on the wrist. Liona is not property. She's everything. She deserves more.

This realization hits me like a wave, and I scoop Liona up in my arms. I carry her out of the spring and down the path to the cottage.

She lies peacefully in my arms, like the first day I claimed her. She's so beautiful, but I know she's not mine. She is hers. I am hers. She can't stay here.

After I put her to bed, I'm getting that potion.

CHAPTER EIGHTEEN

Liona

I'm not sure how long I've been asleep but when I wake up, alone in Beck's bed, my hair is almost completely dry. I must have been knocked out hard because I didn't even notice that Beck left. I guess it's good that I'm alone. It gives me time to register everything that's happened today.

You'd think watching Beck beat another man and then fucking me next to his unconscious body, covered in his blood, would be the part that rattled me, but it's not. That just seemed like the logical outcome for Donny trying to take advantage of me like he did. I've never experienced something so hot in my life and although I hope that's the last time something like that happens, I know I'll revisit it often in my thoughts.

The part that has me shitting bricks is when Beck said he loves me. I should have seen this coming, but it's just been so fun and sexy that I didn't want to cloud my thoughts with the seriousness of our relationship. What even is our relationship? Can a captor and a captive really fall in love?

I get out of bed, stretching to my tippy-toes, and pull one of Beck's cotton shirts over my head. I'm engulfed with Beck's earthy scent that has grown so familiar. I find myself bringing a corner of the shirt up to my nose so that I can breathe him in. I take a moment to assess my body's reaction. A wave of calmness runs over me and I feel lighter. Is this what being in love is like?

Lawrence's face flashes in my mind. It's not that hard to believe I never loved him. Although I tried to bury the thoughts, I knew I agreed to marry him for the security and comfort he offered. Now that I have almost zero of my modern life comforts, I realize that might not be as essential as I thought, and most importantly, it might not be worth marrying someone I don't love.

I'm pacing back and forth around the cottage, wrestling with my thoughts. Is confessing my love and surrendering to stay with Beck just my brain's way of coping with the fact that now I have an excuse to run away from my problems with Lawrence? It's not like I have much of a choice if I stay with Beck or not at this point, but can I honestly say that I love him?

The answer seems clearer to me than I want to believe. I've never felt this feeling before and although it could be a result of me being held captive, I don't really care. I want to lean into this. I want to admit my love for Beck. And there it is. I love him. How stupid of me, but it's true. This all seems like destiny; in some crazy fucked up way, it's like we're meant to be together. It's like he always says, "You were made for me." Well, what if that's the truth?

I'm suddenly giddy, jumping up and down, and I can hardly wait for Beck to get back so I can tell him. I need to do something to calm my nerves, or I'm going to end up ripping apart all my split ends before he arrives.

I rummage around in the kitchen. I think it's time that I made Beck a meal for a change. I honestly have no idea what time it is and what meal would be appropriate. The day took my sense of time out of me. I decide that breakfast would be the best option and start to whip up some pancakes.

Thirty minutes later, Beck comes through the door. Flour is everywhere, and I've burnt the only two pancakes that managed to make it to the griddle over his fire.

"Hi!" I rush towards him and wrap my arms around him, too happy to care about my epic fail of breakfast.

He puts something down on the table and then scoops me up so I can meet him eye to eye. I can't help but notice the look on his face. It's more sober and serious than I'm used to. I think I know why.

"I love you," I whisper and then kiss him.

He's still at first, not reciprocating my passion, but then he leans into it. His lips open up and he matches my tongue's movements. His hand reaches for the back of my head. He walks to the bed and throws me on top.

My senses are alive and I'm throbbing between my legs.

But his body doesn't come crashing down on top of me. "I see you've cooked." An amused grin forms on his face as he turns back and examines the kitchen.

"I tried. Maybe we'll just leave the cooking up to you." I sit up and get to my knees. I crawl toward him and work on unfastening the buttons of his pants. "I can find other ways to repay you."

Beck put his hand over his buttons and then sits next to me. "We need to talk. I shouldn't have said I love you earlier."

I lean over him, grasping his arm. "Beck, didn't you hear me? I love you too! I'm sorry I didn't say it earlier, but I was scared. I'm not scared anymore. I love you."

He stands up and paces back and forth in front of me, his palms pressed against his forehead. "No, Liona. You can't love me. I captured you."

I chuckle and walk toward him. "I know it's a little bit unconventional, but I've thought about it. I really do love you. I never felt this was with Lawrence or anyone before."

He looks me in the eyes. "Is Lawrence your fiancé? You never mention him."

"Yes." I grasp for words. "I never talk about him because I never really loved him. Even before I met you. I was just marrying him because he was rich, and I wanted to be taken care of. Now I know I don't need all of that. I just need you."

He runs his hands through his hair with a pained expression on his face. "You can't stay here, Liona!" he yells, and I take a step back, shocked.

"What are you talking about?" Tears are forming at the corner of my eyes.

He rushes over to the table and picks up a vial. It must have been what he put down when he got in. "This potion will make you forget everything you saw here. I'm going to take you to the edge of the woods and you're going to take it."

"Wha... no...." I'm sobbing now and searching for words.

"Liona, you can't stay here. After what happened with Donny, it made me realize how the others will view you. You deserve a life amongst people that consider you their equal. You won't live a fulfilled life here."

"So you lied to me? You said there was no way I could leave."

He rushes to me and kneels in front of me. "I didn't know this potion existed until recently. One of the younger wizards told me about it when we went into town. I didn't want to tell you because I was falling in love with you, and I didn't want you to leave. Now I know there's no other choice. If I love you, I have to let you go."

Somehow this hurts worse than anything else. He does love me; so much so that he would let me go even though it would hurt him. How can I leave a man like this?

I just stare down at him, tears streaming down my face. I'm angry. He didn't tell me when he found out about the potion, and now he's making me leave right after he confesses his love to me? I don't want to leave and I especially don't want to forget my time with him. I'll make him pay.

The brass key to the cage, the one that Beck locked me in the first night I was here, catches my eye from the kitchen counter. I'll show him I'm not going. I dart for it, grab it off the counter, and rush toward the cage. I slam the door behind me, locking it with the key.

"What are you doing?" Beck stares at me with a confused expression on his face.

"You can't make me leave!" I yell to him.

He gives a pained laugh and then walks over to me. "Liona, you can't stay in the cage forever. Just like you can't stay in this cage of a community forever."

I say nothing. I just sway my hips slightly and play with the hem of Beck's shirt resting on my upper thighs.

Beck's eyes immediately trail to my fingers.

I grab onto the shirt and slowly bring it higher and higher, still swaying my hips.

"What are you doing?" Beck asks, his eyes still on my fingers.

"I'm punishing you." I lick my lips and bring his shirt over my head.

Beck exhales as if in pain. His large hands wrap around the bars of my cage.

I step back. I don't want him to reach me. My hands slide up and down my body. I grab both of my breasts and moan.

"Come on, Liona," Beck begs.

His erection is pressed against his pants as if it's going to rip through.

I trail my hands down my body, playing with the curls at my entrance.

"Liona," Beck moans. He wrings his hands on the bars.

Seeing his reaction gives me a high. I love how much power I have over him, even in a cage. It reminds me of the day after he captured me, when I tried to get him to let me out. This is different. I have the control. I have the key.

I stick one finger inside of me. I'm already soaking wet and I know he can hear me pull in and out. I throw my head back and moan in ecstasy.

"Okay, Liona, that's enough. Let me in so I can fuck you."

I turn my gaze to him as my finger slides up and down. "Not until you say I can stay." I drop to my knees and then rest against the back of the cage. I spread my legs wide, so he can get a view of my finger going in and out of me.

"Liona," he says through gritted teeth. "You can't."

"Then you'll just have to watch," I say through angry, airy gasps.

I begin to moan louder as I increase my speed, circling my clit. My other hand cups my breast while my finger circles my nipple.

I'm not going to come yet. I want to make this as long as possible. I want Beck to pay. I slow down my strokes, close my eyes and roll my head back.

Suddenly, I hear a screeching sound. I open my eyes to find Beck bending the bars back with his bare hands. I'm shocked and I stop touching myself so I don't orgasm just from the sight of it. His green muscles pulse, and the veins bulge from his neck. God, he really wants to fuck me.

Just when I think he can't bend them anymore, he gives a loud grunt and pushes them a little bit further. He sighs and bends over, holding himself up with his hands on his knees. He takes a few labored breaths and turns his attention toward me. His eyes are dark. He almost looks angry, but when he licks his lips, I know exactly what he wants to do to me.

He stands up and walks inside the cage.

Chapter Nineteen

Beck

Liona stopped touching herself, which allows me to have enough self-control to stalk slowly over to her instead of ripping my pants off and pounding into her.

Her eyes are wide and her mouth is parted, breathing heavily.

I take slow steps until I'm standing over her. Animalistic instincts run through my veins. All thoughts of our argument, of my tender love for her, have evaporated. All I feel now is a need to claim her. She pushed me to the edge of my control and now she'll pay. "You've been a bad girl, haven't you?"

She gulps and nods her head in admission.

"What did I say happens to bad girls?" I lean over her, supporting my weight with the bars above her.

She closes her eyes. "We get tied up and fucked," she says, breathing so heavily it's hard for her to get the words out.

I swoop down, collect her in my arms, and throw her over my shoulder. I drop her to the bed and she arches her back and stretches her arms and legs. A soft moan escapes her.

I march to the kitchen and yank open a drawer containing twine. When I storm over to her, she's already made her way to the top of the bed and her arms are thrown over her head.

"Good girl. Now you are behaving." I lean over her and tie her wrists to the beams of the headboard. As I work, she wraps her legs around my waist and tries to pull herself up and grind against me.

"No!" I bark once I'm finished. "You will stay still unless I tell you otherwise."

She bites her lip and closes her eyes.

I take a second to look over her. Her nipples are taut, her skin is covered in goosebumps and her legs writhe together ever so slightly. I've never seen a more perfect sight.

I spread her legs open and stick a finger inside. She moans and her pussy makes way for me effortlessly. She's soaking and I bring my finger up to my mouth and lick off her sweetness. "You're ready for me, good girl."

"Beck, just fuck me," she says with urgency.

"Ah, ah, ah. I'm the one making orders around here. Now you're going to have to wait for it." I bend over and trail my tongue up her inner thigh.

She moans loudly and yanks at her bonds, trying to push her body closer to me.

I take my time, licking closer and closer until I finally bury my face in her sweet folds. I lick up and down, sticking my tongue inside of her and twirling it around at her top. I start off slow but increase my speed, paying attention to her breathing and her body's reactions. I could lick her all day, but before I know it, she's screaming and her body clenches. More of her liquids flood around me, and I lap them up before coming up.

"You taste so fucking good." I crawl to her and hover my body over hers.

She's pulling against her bonds and she arches her body to try to get closer to mine. "Please," she whimpers.

"That's a good girl, using your manners." I pull down my shorts, revealing my rock-hard cock. It's aching to release.

She looks down at it and licks her lips. "Please," she says again. This time with more force.

I spread her legs wider and thrust into her. Her cunt opens up for me perfectly. "Good girl. You're taking me so good." I thrust in and out, starting off slow, holding onto her breasts to support me. I feel her pussy stretch around me, gripping me harder with each thrust. Although I want this to last, since this might be our last time, I can't take it anymore. I thrust faster and deeper until Liona is screaming my name and pulsing around me. I come right after her, feeling as if every cell in my body is alive.

I collapse next to her because if I lay on top of her, she would be crushed. We both lie there, catching our breaths for a moment, when I remember she's still tied up.

I straddle her and look deep into her eyes. Her face is emotionless, searching mine. I work on her bonds and can already see red lines on her wrists. The thought of marking her thrills me but at the same time saddens me to think I've caused her pain. I cup her small hands into mine and bring them to my lips, kissing her marks.

"Does this mean I can stay?" she finally peeps. Her eyes are large and teary.

I sigh. My mind hasn't changed. I love her. I need her, but her life is more important than my needs. "No, Liona. You can't." I feel myself choking up.

Her brow furrows and she wiggles her way out from underneath me. She grabs my shirt off the floor and pulls it over her head. "Fuck you!" she yells before storming out of the door and slamming it behind her.

CHAPTER TWENTY

Liona

Tears soak my cheeks as I stomp through the forest outside of our cottage. Or should I say *Beck's* cottage, since it's clear he doesn't want me here. I know I'm being dramatic. I know Beck is making me leave because he loves me, but it's just so unfair. At first, he says I can't leave and now he says I must. It's like I have no say over anything when it comes to him.

I thought the cage act would make him reconsider. Does the sex feel as good for him as it does for me? How could he experience even a fraction of the pleasure I feel and say he wants no more? My wanting to stay is more than the sex, though, I know that. I love him. Every giant, terrifying part of him, and I want to be with him. Even if love wasn't enough, I think I'd still want to stay. I've been happier here in this quiet, solitary life, than ever before. I used to think that materialistic possessions and status would make me feel accepted, which I always lacked growing up, but I never felt like I fit in living in LA or being with Lawrence and Victoria's friends. I belong here, with Beck. Can't he see that?

My sobs lessen the farther I walk. A good walk has always been a surefire way to clear my head. Walking in nature has always calmed me. The vastness of it makes me realize how small my problems are.

I come to the boulder I stood on to find Beck's cottage. It feels so long ago, but I realize it's only been a few weeks. I pull myself up and sit on top, staring at the nature around me. I think about the woman I was when I was here last. I was confused and desperate, much like I am now, but for very different reasons. My life was void of passion, of purpose, and any vision of myself. All I cared about was survival. I was tired of living a life in fear. A life worried about safety, my next meal, a family. Lawrence was my ticket to comfort. My ticket to happiness. But now I know I was just relying on a man to take care of me instead of finding that security in myself. A thought passes my consciousness — what if I'm just doing the same thing with Beck?

Sure the passion and feelings between us are eclectic, but am I just using him to hide out and not face the problems I left behind? How will I even know if my love for him is real if I don't have a life where I can survive without it? I've been joking with myself about Stockholm Syndrome this entire time, but what if that's exactly what I'm experiencing? Even as I think this, a part of me fights back. I love him, I do, but how can I ever know for sure?

"Liona!"

I'm not sure what direction the noise is coming from. I stand up on the boulder and look around.

"Liona!"

It doesn't sound like Beck's husky and boisterous voice, but it has to be him. Maybe the distance between us is distorting the sound.

"I'm right here!" I yell with my hands cupping my mouth.

"Liona!"

They're getting closer.

From my elevated spot, I see something rustle from the brush in the distance. I strain my eyes until I see a man emerge into a clearing. He has short blonde hair and a slender build. He's wearing a long sleeve shirt with a vest. "Liona!" he calls, and this time I can make out the voice and put it with a face.

It's Lawrence.

CHAPTER TWENTY-ONE

Liona

"What are you doing here?" I don't even realize the words pass my lips. I'm shocked and I feel as if I'm floating outside of my body.

"What am I doing here? What are *you* doing here? I've been looking everywhere for you! Did you just run off on your bachelorette trip and decide to rough it in the woods?" Lawrence seems more mad than glad to have found me, but he gives me a hug, patting my back after five seconds.

I reach out and touch his face, just to make sure he's real and not a figment of my imagination. I've never seen him in clothes like these. Although I can tell they're expensive, they're casual outdoorsy clothes. They look so new and clean, I wonder how he even got this far in the woods without getting them dirty. "How did you find me?" I ask, still in awe.

"I tracked your phone." He holds up his to show me the GPS page.

That makes sense. I know that even if your phone dies, it will still show its location the last time it was on. I don't even know where my phone is, but it has to be around here somewhere.

"Why did it take you so long to find me?" Except for the first few nights, I haven't really cared if anyone searched for me. In fact, I didn't think anyone would. I'm aware of the shallow pool of my relationships.

"You wrote a note that said to not come find you. Victoria and the girls wanted to give you some space."

Oh yeah, shit.

"Besides, I was in Hong Kong on business. I had to wait until I got back."

There it is.

Lawrence examines me like I'm a wild animal. "What are you doing? Whose clothes are you wearing? Did you run away to live in the woods?"

I'm not sure which of his questions to answer first. "Uh, yeah," is all I manage to say.

"Well, you're filthy, and normal people just get a pill cocktail when they have a nervous breakdown, not hide out like Bigfoot."

"Noted." I stare at him and feel nothing. I don't even care that he's obviously repulsed by me or thinks I'm crazy. I don't care what he thinks.

He sighs and under his breath says, "I was worried."

My ice cold heart melts just a tiny bit. It wasn't like Lawrence just confessed his undying love for me or told me I'm the most beautiful thing in the world, but for Lawrence, telling me he was worried about me is a lot. He's usually all business. No emotions. Maybe he does actually care for me, even a little.

I stand there for a second, neither of us saying anything. "Okay... well, are you ready to go back now?" He turns to start walking the way he came.

I look back. I can't see the cottage from this far, but the unmistakable presence of Beck beckons me. Can I really just leave without saying goodbye?

But Beck wants me gone. If I tell Lawrence no, I'll just be delaying the inevitable and then I'll have nowhere to go. Besides, Beck will only let me go if I take his brain-erasing potion. Even though it hurts like a mother fucker that Beck doesn't want me to stay, I don't want to forget about him. I need something to think about if I end up marrying Lawrence and am subjected to his lackluster love making for the rest of my life. I also want to know if what I feel for Beck is real. Maybe time apart from him is the only way to tell.

I can't believe I'm even considering this. After everything – all the feelings I've felt, after all the voids have been filled. How can I just go back and pretend none of it happened? But what other choice do I have?

I turn back to Lawrence. "Okay, I'm ready."

CHAPTER TWENTY-TWO

Liona

Getting used to my life back in LA is much harder than I thought. The minute Lawrence and I arrived at LAX and I stepped outside the airport to the bustling city, I felt like some Tarzan character who lived their whole lives talking to animals. Had it always been this loud? Had there always been this many people? I didn't think I could handle it, but once we made it back to Lawrence's sterile and quiet apartment, I felt a little sense of normalcy. I did miss electricity, television, and indoor plumbing. Although I was sure I never wanted to set foot outside again, it felt kind of good to be back to my life.

Lawrence has been giving me my space, which I'm thankful for. I can tell that he senses I'm not the same person as when I left. He hasn't asked me any questions about where I've stayed or why I even "ran away," which is great because I don't think I have it in me to tell him I got captured by an ogre that I've been fucking on the regular. Also, I think if I divulge that information to anyone, the magical community will murder me, literally. But more likely, Lawrence will think I've gone insane and admit me to a mental hospital. I can tell he's already thinking about it, and I don't want to encourage him.

I've been back for two weeks, and I spend most of my days journaling. I just want to get everything that happened down on paper and out of the tangled mess of my mind. I keep trying to piece it all together. I want to map out the minute my attraction for Beck started and decipher if the feelings I had were true. The problem is that every time I try to record the sex acts, I end up getting so horny that I have to touch myself and completely abandon my journaling. My self-actualization is going tremendously slow, and I don't think I've actually uncovered anything. Except for the fact that I am still very much sexually attracted to Beck, even with the distance and time between us. I don't even want to think about if it's more than that.

Most nights I spend silently crying. I hate myself for it and luckily Lawrence is such a heavy sleeper he doesn't even notice. I don't know why I cry. I can't tell if it's just the immense shock to my system after being kidnapped and stripped from the life I knew or the shock of returning back to everything. Or if it's because my heart is ripped in two. One piece is with me in LA and the other is in the swamps of Florida. As time moves on, I know it's probably the latter.

Lawrence and I have decided to go through with the wedding. Well, I wouldn't say *we* decided, more like we haven't talked about it at all, and he keeps paying deposits to the wedding planner to make things happen. I know I shouldn't do it. If anything, my time with Beck showed me that I shouldn't be getting married to Lawrence, but everything is just too much right now. It's easier to just go with the flow and continue to let Lawrence handle it. I know I'm chicken shit, but I couldn't give less of a fuck at this point. My sole purpose for existence recently is to live a comfortable, stress-free life. It makes the pain I've been feeling these last two weeks more bearable.

Today, I woke up feeling more like myself. Lawrence kissed me on the cheek before heading off to work, and I decided to start my day with a walk through my neighborhood. Although the noises pounded in my head, I started to notice the little things that made me fall in love with LA in the first place. The people with smiles on their faces, the artisan coffee shops on every corner, the art that covers every open wall – all little pieces that make the city so exciting.

I kick my sneakers off when I step through our doorway and see my cell phone on the counter has a missed text from Victoria.

"Hi, girl, Lawrence told me you're back. Hope you're okay. I'd love to catch up soon. Let me know when you can hang."

This brings a smile to my face. Although Victoria is usually a pain in the ass, and she drove me crazy during my shit show of a bachelorette party, she is my friend nonetheless and, most importantly, my future sister-in-law. I should try harder to be a better friend to her.

My stomach grumbles, and a brilliant idea pops into my head. I can pick up some lunch at my favorite sushi burrito place for Victoria and me. Surprising her with lunch is just the kind of thing I need to do to make up for being a shitty, runaway friend.

Half an hour later, I'm taking the elevator up to her apartment building, poke bowls in hand. It's nice that we live so close to each other, and I really should make it a point to visit her more.

When I get to her door, I pull the handle. I've never been a knocking type. "Surprise! I brought you lunch!" I bellow as I swing open the door.

I hear Victoria scream from her bedroom.

"Sorry! I know I should knock, but I feel like the forced entry adds to the surprise."

"Shit!" comes from the bedroom.

Oops, maybe I caught her at a bad time.

I walk to the kitchen and put the bowls on the counter, watching the door of her room.

Seconds later, Victoria emerges in a robe with her hair disheveled. "Liona, what are you doing here?" She seems pissed.

"I... I just thought it would be nice to surprise you with lunch. Is someone here with you?"

"No!" she says, way too fast.

A tumble comes from her room and I raise an eyebrow at her.

"Look, Liona, this is a bad time. I'll call you and we can schedule drinks soon. I'm sorry to push you out but..."

"No, it's okay. I got it. I'm sorry for surprising you." I turn to leave, completely abandoning the poke bowls, when something catches my eye, a man's shoes by the front door. I bought those shoes. They were custom-made, flannel-lined Prada loafers I got for Lawrence's birthday.

"Did your brother leave his shoes here?" I whip around and look at Victoria in the hallway. Of course, that's the only logical explanation, but her face says otherwise. She looks... guilty.

"Uh... oh yeah. I think so." She's sweating.

What would she be suspicious about concerning Lawrence?

Unless...no.

I storm past her and walk to her bedroom.

"Liona, wait. You can't go in there." She grabs at my arm, trying to pull me back, but her tiny Pilates arms are no match for me.

I reach the door and throw it open.

Lawrence is sitting on the edge of Victoria's bed, only wearing boxers.

Neither of them says anything, but they don't have to. I can read it all over their similar-looking faces.

WHAT.

THE.

FUCK.

A ringing goes off in my head. I feel like I'm floating outside of my body. I just stand there.

Victoria pushes past me and stands next to Lawrence. "Please, Liona, we can explain."

"Okay. Then do," I say without moving an inch.

Victoria's mouth is parted, her eyes are bulging, and she looks to Lawrence, unable to find the words.

Lawrence sighs and then speaks. "Okay, maybe it's exactly what it looks like."

"So, you're fucking your sister," I say matter-of-factly, not letting any emotions show. The history of the two flood my brain. Every interaction they had, every time I thought they were a little too close for comfort. Even though I always thought their relationship was weird, I *never* could actually imagine this.

"Half-siblings, actually," Victoria says meekly.

I scoff. "Oh, well, in that case, how fucking adorable!" Here comes the rage. I turn around and run toward the door. I am suffocating, and I can't take a minute more of this Alabama freak show. I'm not even jealous or sad, just completely repulsed.

"Liona, wait!" Lawrence catches up with me in the kitchen and grabs my arm. "Victoria and I aren't in love. We just know each other's bodies better than anyone else. It's purely physical."

"Are you trying to make me puke? How the fuck did you expect that to make me feel better?" I try to get away, but he grabs harder.

"We can make this work. Don't pretend that you enjoy fucking me. We can get married, have kids, and we can both fuck whomever we want. Come on, don't pretend that you weren't shacking up with some guy when I found you. You were wearing a man's shirt. You would never have survived in the wilderness on your own."

"I could have fucked an entire football team, and it wouldn't even hold a candle to the fact that you are having sex with your sister!"

I hear Victoria sob from the bedroom.

"Grow the fuck up." He pushes me away and perches onto the back of the couch. He folds his hands and stares at me. "I treat you like a goddamn queen and ask nothing of you. When I found you, you had nothing! I gave you everything. All you have to do is marry me and keep your pretty mouth shut and you could have everything you want. Is that really too hard for you?

"Yes, Lawrence. It is too hard for me. I'd rather be married to a man-eating monster than someone who thinks this is okay."

I turn to walk away.

"Liona!" he screams.

I've never heard Lawrence raise his voice. I turn.

"If you so much as speak a word of this to anyone, you'll be wiped off the face of the Earth. Do you hear me? You've only seen a dent into how far our money goes." His eyes are dark and steady, and I can see just how serious he is.

"Fuck you." I walk out the door, but then open it again and stick my head in. "And fuck you too, Victoria."

Chapter Twenty-Three

Liona

It hasn't even been a month since I discovered I was engaged to an incestual asshole, but I've already moved out of his palace of an apartment and into a shithole of a studio apartment above a Chinese restaurant.

If I wasn't sure before if I should marry Lawrence or not, it's become abundantly clear. He can threaten me all he wants, but I refuse to marry someone who fucks their sister, and I don't think that's such a crazy thought.

I haven't cried over him, not even a single tear. I try to block out all thoughts of him before the bile rises from my stomach. Although I'm not glad that I discovered what I did, it felt like a weight was lifted off my shoulders. I don't have to marry Lawrence. Nothing is wrong with me for not loving him. I can be on my own.

I've already gotten a new job at a local breakfast spot, and I have to say, I enjoy working again. I'm back to struggling, back to living paycheck to paycheck, but there's something so liberating about not having to rely on anyone but myself. I don't know why I spent so much time afraid of this. I'm finally free.

I can't deny that the freedom is cloaked with a wave of loneliness. Not for the sake of being lonely or because of everything I lost with the sliver of positivity I had with Lawrence. No, I'm lonely for one person only. Of course, that person is an ogre. My ogre. Beck.

Time away from him has just confirmed that my love for him was real. *Is* real. Although I love being on my own and supporting myself, I would give up everything to be with him again, but I know that can't be. Not only do we have the barrier of being different species, but we also have the boulder of obstacles that include our distance, his community, and the unconventional start of our relationship. It's all too complicated and impossible to work. Even if we could find a way together, there's still the fact that he will never find me. Sure, I could travel to him, but I'm so poor I can't afford to fly all the way back to Florida.

Every night, before I go to bed, I toss and turn and imagine a future where I do have enough money to travel back to him. Maybe we can figure out a plan together, but for right now, those maybes have to live in my dreams, and boy, those dreams already mean so much to me.

Tonight is no different. I lie awake, staring at the stained ceiling above my bed. I think about Beck's face. It feels so long since I've seen him last. I try to concentrate on the image of his angular jaw, his pearly white fangs, and the thick brows that covered his hazel eyes. My imagination draws down to his chest, so built and wide. Although his muscles are hard as rocks, his skin is warm and silky. What I would give to be wrapped up in his arms again. Then his dick comes to mind. It's one I know I'll never be able to find again. He always said I was made for him, which has to be true. His cock fit inside of me like it was molded from my core, stretching me out and hitting my G-spot every time.

My fingers trail underneath my nightgown. Most nights end up like this, getting off at just the thought of Beck. It will never be enough, though. Sometimes the thought of that makes me cry, but tonight is not the night for tears, I don't think I have enough moisture in my body from how wet I already feel.

A bang comes from my front door. I yank my hands to my comforter and pull the blankets in front of me as if they are a shield.

"Who is it?" I yell, hoping that someone accidentally got the wrong apartment. My heart is beating outside of my chest.

No answer, but the bangs continue. Whoever it is trying to get through the door.

I've always thought that if push came to shove, I'd be a boss-ass bitch. I'd swing into action, grab as many knives as possible from my kitchen and go full ninja mode onto some prick's punk ass. But at this moment, I'm completely paralyzed. I've been so happy with my decisions and that I'm living on my own terms, but now, I hate that I've allowed myself to be in such a dangerous situation. I live in a dangerous part of town alone, and now some scary-ass mother fucker is pounding my door down to murder me and steal my shit, or worse.

"Go away!" I yell as my last feeble attempt to deter my murderer before burying my head in my covers and hiding in plain sight.

The door slams open.

My body is shaking no matter how hard I try to still myself. Maybe if he can't find me, he'll just take my shit and leave. Maybe he'll just completely ignore the fact that my scratchy voice yelled from the other side of the door he just pounded down. Maybe it's actually a unicorn that shits hundred-dollar bills. The possibilities are endless. I know, though. I'm getting killed. RIP me.

Thunderous footsteps approach closer. My hand's over my mouth, trying to silence my breath. Tears fall from the corners of my eyes. The steps stop next to my bed, and the blankets are pulled from over my head.

I remain still, waiting for whatever will happen next. God, I'm such a little bitch.

"Liona."

I'd know that voice anywhere. I flip over and face the man standing over my bed.

"Beck!"

CHAPTER TWENTY-FOUR

Beck

"You asshole!" Liona sits up and chucks a pillow at my head.

I yank off my face mask and pull down my hood. "Liona, I can explain." I'm grasping for her. The need to hold her in my arms is overwhelming.

"Couldn't you just knock on the door like a normal person? You scared the shit out of me!" Her brow is furrowed and her cheeks hold a blush.

I stalk closer to her and lean over her bed, supporting myself with my outstretched arms. My heart is beating out of my chest. It's been almost two months since I've seen her last, and every day has been agony. I need her, and I don't have time for words. "I'm not a normal person. I'm an ogre. I couldn't wait another second for you to open that door. I can smell your arousal, Liona. If I don't have my cock buried deep inside of you in the next five minutes, I think I might die." The rational part of my brain knows that this is not how it's supposed to go. There's a lot of explaining that we both need to do and things to talk out, but Liona is my drug. Rationality can come later. Now, I just need her.

Liona's illuminated by a dim lamp next to her bed. Her lips are parted, letting out heavy breaths, and her breasts rise and fall under her satin nightgown. She just stares at me for a moment.

"Oh my God, just fuck me." She removes the space between us, wrapping her arms around my neck and meeting my lips.

My mouth devours her, and I lean her back into the bed, supporting her neck with my hand. "Liona," I moan into her mouth.

Her arms move down my chest unzipping my hoodie and pulling it off of me.

I rip the straps of her nightgown and pull it down, exposing her full, round tits.

Liona gives a sob as my hand grabs her. My other hand reaches for my pants, yanking them down and releasing my aching cock.

The moment it's free, Liona scoots down from under me and grabs it.

A chill runs down my spine. "I need you, Liona."

She positions my head at her entrance.

I try to reach down and touch her. Even though I could smell her from the hallway, I want to make sure she's ready for me.

She swats my hand away and wraps her legs around mine, impaling herself on my dick. I slide in easily. She's as eager to have me inside her as I am.

She cries out with each thrust, and her moans speed up as I increase my speed.

This is not how I planned our reunion. I planned to explain my feelings to her, kiss every inch of her body, and make this first time after so long last as long as I could, but the monster inside of me can't wait. It seems like Liona's monster is unable to control herself as well.

Our moans melt together until our bodies tense, and we both come undone. I feel as if I can finally breathe for the first time in weeks. I feel whole and empty in the best way.

I lie beside her while we catch our breaths, tracing circles on her dewy stomach. "Why did you leave?" I finally ask.

She turns her head to look at me, her face scrunched in utter confusion. "You wanted me to leave." She sits up and stares down at me.

"I wanted to keep you safe, not have you leave without saying goodbye."

"What would goodbyes do, Beck? Would goodbyes make us forget about each other? I know your stupid potion would, but is that what you really want? To forget about me?" She gets out of bed and stands over me.

I press the palms of my hands to my forehead. "Liona, I love you. I want what's best for you. How can you be happy in my swamp?"

"It's not just a swamp. It's a swamp with you. How can I be happy with anything less?"

I turn my body and stare at her. She's so beautiful when she's angry. Her cheeks are flushed and her eyes hold a steely expression. I love her so much, but how can we be together?

She breaks the moment of silence. "Why are you here then? Are you here to give me that potion?"

I sit up. "No!" I don't want to force you to take something you don't want. I've already told the board you took it. I just...I couldn't take it anymore. I wasn't thinking clearly. I just had to find you."

"And how did you find me? How did you even get here without being noticed?"

"Winston. The wizard who gave me the potion. He was able to track you. I put on a hoodie, some sunglasses, and a facemask and took a plane. No one noticed me."

She nods. "Well, you found me. Was this enough for you? Was one last fuck enough for us to be apart forever?" Tears are now streaming down her face.

I sit on the edge of the bed and gather her in my arms. I look into her eyes. "No, it will never be enough. I could be with you every second for the rest of my life, and it will still never be enough."

"Then how can you not take me back then?"

"I don't want to capture you again. I want to do what's best for you."

She sits up on my lap and faces me, her naked body presses against me. "Beck, I've had enough time away from you. I've seen life without you, and I don't want it. This is my choice. I want to be with you, no matter what obstacles come our way."

My dick is pounding, but I fight my sexual urges and try to focus on her words. She's right. How could this ever end? She loves me and I love her. I can't keep fighting this. When I planned to come here, this is exactly what I hoped would happen, whether I want to admit it or not.

"Okay," I surrender.

"Okay?" A smile forms on her face.

"Okay." I shrug and smirk.

"So, I can come back with you?

"Yes, but on one condition."

Her face sobers. "What's that?"

"You have to sit on my face before we go."

She laughs and bites her lip before scooting up my thighs. "Oh, there's a lot of things we need to do before we go." She pushes me back on the bed and covers my body with hers.

I don't think we'll be making it back to the swamp anytime soon.

CHAPTER TWENTY-FIVE

Liona

The sun warming my cheeks feels like a gentle kiss, urging me to wake up. I rub my eyes and turn to face the window. A smile spreads across my face as I stare at my ogre, sleeping peacefully next to me.

Every morning starts out like this, ever since I moved back into Beck's cottage. I've missed my morning trips to the bodega to get a breakfast sandwich, but other than that, everything is better at the swamp. I've settled back into my quiet lifestyle and have found so much joy in my day-to-day routines. Beck and I go into town often. Beck made a proclamation of his love to me during the last town meeting and let everyone know that if anyone thought of me other than Beck's equal, they wouldn't be as fortunate as Donny, who still bares the scars of Beck's warning. Since then, everyone treats me like a completely normal person, or should I say, a normal magical creature. I know it's just because they're scared shitless of Beck, but honestly, that's hot as fuck. Life has been good.

I take a big stretch and scoot over as close as I can to Beck. I don't touch him yet. I just want to stare at his immaculate form for just a few moments longer. You would think that after the two months back living with him, I would get used to looking at him, but I don't think I ever will. Part of it is that he's an ogre, but most of it is that he's so fucking hot.

My staring only lasts a few moments before I can't take it anymore. I press my body up against his, and his arms tighten around me.

He's so hard, especially his dick. "Good morning." He smiles with his eyes still closed.

"Hi," I say before kissing his face. I trail down his neck. I feel his morning wood becoming even harder against my body. I keep moving lower and lower, letting my tongue drag against his green, delicious skin.

His breath heavies until I get to the spot above his pelvis. "Oh fuck." He moans.

I throw the covers off of us and sit up so I can glimpse his manhood. My mouth waters at the sight of it. I lean over and lick his head. Drops of precum trickle into my mouth, and I swear nothing has tasted so good. I roll my lips over his top and slowly swallow him deep. When I reach the base of his shaft, he gives a shuddering moan. I come up for air. "I want you to fuck my face."

He doesn't hesitate. He sits up and gathers my hair in his fist. I swallow him again, and Beck starts to thrust inside of me. At first, he starts out slow and shallow. I try to pull against him to go deeper, but he just yanks my hair back. "Na ah ah, you asked me to fuck you. Let me do the fucking." His words send a shiver down my body.

He starts to increase his speed and go deeper down my throat. Of course, I've had a lot of practice taking him in my mouth. If not, I don't think he would be able to fuck my throat so deep without me choking. I gag, and tears fall from the corner of my eyes, but he knows this is what I like. He doesn't stop. He pounds me harder and deeper until I feel his body tense, and he bursts inside of me, filling my mouth. I swallow him up and lick the remaining drops from his head.

It doesn't even take a second for Beck to pull me up to him and press his lips against mine. He kisses me as if he's starving and when he comes up for air, he confirms that thought. "Sit on my face. It's my turn to eat."

How can I say no to that?

He lays down on his back, and I crawl until my cunt is over his mouth. His tongue is so large that in one swipe, it reaches me from my back to front. He holds my thighs up a bit to say, "Ride my face."

I comply and begin to grind my body up and down against his glorious tongue. Beck doesn't slow down but focuses in on my clit with immense concentration until I'm writhing and screaming his name at the top of my lungs.

My body convulses and I roll over to my side.

Beck licks his lips and turns on his side to face me. He stares down at me and strokes the side of my face.

I look into his eyes, taking in the warm sparkle that they hold. God, do I love this man.

I break our mushy staring contest. "I know we just ate, but I'm actually feeling hungry after exerting that much energy."

Beck gives a deep laugh. "Of course you are." He leans over and kisses me tenderly, cupping my face.

It's so crazy, but I feel myself getting wet again. We could stay in bed all day and just fuck each other until we're a pile of mush, but we'd probably starve if we let ourselves indulge. I pull away, knowing exactly what will happen if I lean in anymore.

Beck sighs and nods, as if he understands my silent thoughts. "Okay. Why don't you take a shower? I'm making waffles."

He hops from bed, and I stare at his perfect backside. I grab a pillow and press it over my face to suppress my moan. To think my only discomfort in life is the fact that I have to stop myself from spending all day jumping Beck's bones.

Damn, life is good. Life is good.

Read the next book, *Stay In My Swamp: An Ogre Happily Ever After*

Thanks for reading!

Thank you for reading! If you liked *Get In My Swamp: An Ogre Love Story*, please make sure to leave a review on Amazon and Goodreads.

Want more of G.M. Fairy? Check out her next books...

Stay In My Swamp: An Ogre Happily Ever After
Book 2: Life in the swamp can't get any better for Liona and Beck. That's until Beck pops a big question that forces Liona to face some unfinished business. She heads back to LA but Beck isn't too far behind, this time looking less like an ogre thanks to some help from Winston the Wizard.

Will magic be enough for Beck to get Liona to stay in his
swamp forever?

Spellbound Seduction: A Wizard Love Story

Book 3 and Standalone: Winston the Wizard is a master of magic but a stranger to love. He's lived a full life in the hidden world of the magical community but lives with a condition that makes it impossible to connect fully. He's content with his life as the manager of Happily Ever Endings, a club for adult enchantments, until he meets Marigold— a young woman who suffers from a similar condition, and she needs his help to cope with it. Winston feels an instant connection with her but knows they can never be. Can he overcome his fears and help her find happiness? Or will he lose her to the curse that haunts them both? Find out in this spellbinding romance of magic and mystery.

My AI: A Robot Why-Choose Love Story

After social media star Azzy, has a very public panic attack at a red-carpeted award show, her best friend orders her an Andro Corp. Bodyguard. When her robot bodyguard gets delivered, Azzy quickly realizes Model REM082 is the man of her dreams. Things start heating up as Remmy, as she likes to call him, becomes more and more sentient and does whatever it takes to please her.

Stay up to date on all things G.M. Fairy....

Made in United States
North Haven, CT
31 July 2023

39624845R00117